THE PROFESSOR

THE PROFESSOR

A Novel

By

REX WARNER

faber and faber

This edition first published in 2008
by Faber and Faber Ltd
3 Queen Square, London WC1N 3AU

A CIP record for this book is available from the British Library

ISBN 978-0-571-24318-1

CONTENTS

PAGE

To
G. J. S. W.

THE PROFESSOR

CHAPTER I

THEORISTS

THE last week enjoyed, or rather experienced, by Professor A may be reconstructed with tolerable accuracy from two sources—from the Professor's intimate diary, rediscovered at a much later date than that of the events with which it deals, and from the verbal evidence of his son There is also the indirect evidence of one or two other survivors

Those who knew the man seem to have admired him, though pity rather than admiration is likely to be the feeling by which those who peruse his history will be most affected, for we shall see a man quite unfitted for power, in his day the greatest living authority on Sophocles, rich in the culture of many languages and times, but for his own time, not through irresolution or timidity but rather, as it seems to us, through a pure kind of blindness, most inapt He believed against all the evidence, scholar though he was, not only in the existence but in the efficacy of a power more human, liberal, and kindly than an organization of metal He believed not simply in the utility but in the over-ridmg or pervasive power of the disinterested reason Metal was to be proved haider than his flesh, stupidity and fanaticism more influential than his gentlest syllogisms, and yet, easy though it is to name the man a pedant and dismiss him as misguided, his contribution to a civilization that may one day be oigamzed or given room to flower will be found, perhaps, to have been not altogether *nil*

Let us imagine, then, the last Monday of the Professor's life At ten o'clock in the morning of this day he was standing on the dais of the College Hall, his long fingers turning over the pages of the text of Œdipus Tyrannus, and apparently unaware of the fifty or sixty students, men and women, who were crowding to their places at tables below the dais, sharpening pencils, smoothing out note-books, smiling, nodding, conversing together in low tones The Professor looked up from the pages

of his book and immediately his audience became attentive
Even the most stupid, the Professor knew, would pretend to be
interested in his lectures, a tribute perhaps to his ability, perhaps
to his charm, perhaps to his European reputation as a scholar
Yet of late the Professor had remarked a slight change in the
attitude towards him of his students, and he was by no means
satisfied with the change It was not that they listened less
intently to his words, still less was there any sign of what
happened, he knew, sometimes during the lectures of some of
his colleagues, open insubordination and plainly expressed
dissatisfaction with the arguments or conclusions of a lecturer
Many people indeed would have been flattered rather than
perplexed by the complete silence that he commanded and the
steady upturned faces which he now saw before him But the
Professor felt uneasily that, although his words were being
heard attentively, it was he himself who was most closely
scrutinized While he aimed, with his genuine enthusiasm and
deep scholarship, to give others the technical equipment and the
sensitiveness by which they, as well as he, might enjoy what he
regarded as the highest intellectual achievements of mankind,
he dimly knew, and was ill at ease, that his audience were, at the
best, only half interested in seizing the opportunities with which
he was providing them Those faces, some keen, some sullen,
but all attentive, were judging not so much the poems of
Sophocles as the critic of the poems, and judging him not as a
critic, but as a man

For some time now the Professor's name had been mentioned
in the Press as the possible head of a Government of National
concentration Where else, it had been asked, could such
another man be found? A man whose name was known and
respected all over Europe, a man whose integrity no one had
ever questioned or could ever question, a man who had shown
himself in his speeches and writings to be able to understand
the best aims of all parties and yet who was attached to none,
a man who could be relied upon to uphold, or, if necessary, to
modify the constitution only by the recognized processes of
law, one whom neither brow-beating, cajolery nor false alarms
would be likely to turn from a course of the strictest honesty
and widest sympathy Was he the strong man? some questioned,
and to these the Professor's supporters had a ready answer
It was true that the enemy on the frontier could dispose of a
vast army, overwhelming forces of men and metal, was it not

also true that only the combined action of the country's foreign allies could deter the enemy from an invasion that during the last few years had been now more now less threatening, but always possess? And what public figure did they possess more certain to inspire confidence and respect abroad than the Professor?

As for the Professor himself, he knew well enough how his name was bandied about the streets That very day he was expecting a message from the Chancellory What was disquietening to him now was the fact that these young men and women at the University, to whom he would have wished to be simply a teacher and a friend, were regarding him already as a public figure, some with hope, some with dissatisfaction, some, it seemed to him, with a kind of contempt That they should be enthusiastic about politics was understandable enough, and even admirable, it was understandable, too, though less to be admitted that, in the present situation, this enthusiasm should seem bitter and boundless

Yet now he was lecturing on Sophocles Why could they not, if even for a few moments, open their minds to the divine flow of verse and with him enter a world unlike their own, a world where emotion was deeply felt, clearly defined and energetically expressed? Let them by all means be studious of and dogmatic in politics. (though how many, he wondered, of these boys and girls had made any study either of economics or of political theory?), but let them at least own the existence and the importance of that other world inhabited still by ghosts greater than the living and able still to live as a source of inspiration or comfort in despair

He saw his son, sitting, at one of the tables in the middle of the hall, and reflected sadly that this boy, probably the most promising of all his pupils, was now spending the greater part of his time in political work It was natural, no doubt, he thought, and yet his face lacked something of its usual undisturbed calm as he glanced quickly away from the upturned faces and down to the page in front of him

"Line 102" he said and, looking rather over the students' heads in the direction of the back of the hall, he began in his musical gentle voice to pronounce the Greek words

ὡς οὐδέν ἐστιν οὔτε πυργος οὔτε ναῦς
ἔρημος ἀνδρῶν μὴ ζυνοικουντων ἔσω

And before two or three syllables had been spoken, such was the effect On him of the language he had learnt to love, that his mind became momentarily as remote from the College Hall and the agitated streets outside as if he himself had been a character in some different period of history or a figure in a legend He was in that world, half of fact and half of fancy, where he could survey at once a hundred cities or islands dancing in the golden sea. Over the waves skimmed the care-free halcyons, and the grey water was frothed to whiteness by the stern oars of heroes returning, for the most part, to trouble or disaster There were hundreds of ships visible from a golden throne; in a tent was the savage beauty and huge shadow of a warrior stretching out in a late compassion his terrible killing hands There was a stocky ungainly figure going to and fro in sunwashed streets, "our comrade, the best man we knew, also the wisest and most just" There were dances along the ridges of the hills, the harsh voices of the sellers of leeks or fish, plague, runners with tremendous news whether of victory or of defeat

The Professor's eyes dropped to the faces in front of him He translated "Since neither tower nor ship is worth anything without men, the men who should be within them," and before his mind's eye there appeared more distinctly a separate scene in rocky country a band of hopelessly defeated men, the remains of two fleets, each considered invincible, but now either sunk or captured, while the men themselves can Hardly escape slavery unless by death They are being exhorted by an elderly general, proved incompetent, but who must know that the situation is hopeless.

The Professor put down the book on the table and stepped forward to the edge of the dais He spoke gently and deliberately. His eyes, too, behind the pince-nez, were calm and gentle, but strangely bright with a boyish enthusiasm whenever, as now, his sympathy or his understanding was deeply engaged "When we read these words," he said, "we can hardly fail to be reminded of very similar words spoken in a quite different situation I am referring, of course, to the last sentence of Nicias' final and desperate appeal to the defeated Athenians in Sicilyddd, ἄνδρες γὰρ πόλις, καὶ οὐ τείχη οὐδὲ νῆες ἀνδρῶν κεναί—'men, constitute a state, not walls or ships that are unmanned.' Indeed the ships of Athens were already lost, and not many years were to pass before her walls, too, would be destroyed How magnificent and generous, at such a moment, to proclaim that fundamentally Athens was the Athenians, that every state or city is the men who make it up! May I be allowed to digress for a moment in order to explain a little more clearly what the Greeks meant by their word 'Polis,' a word which we must translate as 'state' or 'city' Perhaps 'city' is the better translation, for in modern times the state often signifies an organization that is in some way divided from or set above the citizens The Greek Polis, which probably in its original sense meant 'an enclosed space,' was very much more of an organism than is the much larger modern state, or the much less self-conscious modern city There was a conscious community among the citizens of the Polis, rather different, I think, from our modern national patriotism which, whatever its force, would seem to a Greek to contain some elements of artificiality The citizen of Athens was quite consciously in his own life developing and safeguarding a new form of civilization He called it democracy, and his conscious experiment, lasting for barely a hundred years, has, with all its failures and imperfections, profoundly affected the history of the world To-day we can see clearly enough the causes, both internal and external, which brought about the collapse of the Greek Polls It is perhaps more difficult for us to emulate the achievements, whether in living or in art, of those first citizens in Europe The Polis was, let me repeat, an enclosure, a safety zone, or outpost against what to the Greeks (and in a very real sense their view was correct) was actually the barbarism of others who were outside this on the whole liberal organization "

A young man, the Professor's son, rose suddenly in the middle of the hall "Stop! Stop!" he shouted "For God's sake, stop!" Other students were on their feet, though the majority sat staring in amazement at the interrupter A tall young man, whose pale face was flushed with anger, ran across the hall to the Professor and, looking from side to side at father and at son, shouted "Let's throw him out, sir Let's throw him out at once"

The Professor raised his hand and obtained silence "There is evidently some reason for such an interruption," he said "Let us hear what he has to say"

The tall young man bowed before going to his place "All right, sir," he said "Only I demand to be heard afterwards"

The Professor was' surprised "Demand" was a word that he rarely used himself He looked more closely at the young

man and remembered that he had seen him a day or two ago
parading the streets in the uniform, half cowboy, half scout, of
the National Legion "By all means," he said, "let us hear
both sides."

His son was still standing up He showed no longer by any
movement of his body the agitation of mind which had forced
him to make the interruption, but his eyes were almost feverishly
bright and he stood stiff and taut. "I apologize," he said, "for
shouting out as I did. May I say that I was suddenly overwhelmed by one or two thoughts. While you were talking I
saw in front of my eyes the thousands of dead and shattered
bodies of those who have been killed from the air in the towns
and villages of a neighbouring country Those men and women
and children knew nothing of the Polis, had never read Homer,
but had heard of democracy and were pitilessly and brutally
bombed And we, and every democracy in Eurppe, connived
at that slaughter Then I seemed to see our own frontiers, with
a million soldiers, with tanks, guns, and aeroplanes waiting on
the other side, waiting for the easy conquest that can be assured
by a word from our own capital, from our own leaders, to
betray our own people And we are here now, in as desperate
a position as were ever Nicias' soldiers, talking beautifully
about the Polls and enclosed spaces, outposts in which civilization is fostered I wish to disclose the horrible fact that there
is no enclosed space in Europe The enemies of democracy are
in control of our democracies, the enemies of the people rule,
flatter, and bribe the people, our barbarians are both inside
and outside our imagined defences And you, my father, with
all your wisdom, sympathy and culture are, however little you
may like the idea, helping to destroy us Your understanding of
humanity is so great that you can find a hard word for no one
I lack your understanding I have only love And because I
love I hate Please forgive me I know my ignorance but I can
see our danger The word 'Polis' suddenly seemed unfamiliar
to me, in fact terrible, like a joke over a dying man."

He sat down hurriedly as though he wished now to escape
from the attention which he had aroused The Professor
looked with sympathy, and some distress, at his son's ordinary
face, now calm and almost indifferent, beneath his untidy ginger
hair He was about to speak, but observed that the tall young
man, the Legionary, was already on his feet He motioned to

him to begin, and the young man bowed again before speaking in a cold precise voice, choosing his words carefully.

"First of all," he said, "I should like in the name of what I am sure is the majority of those present to express to you, Professor, our deep regret that such an unpleasant incident as that which has just taken place should have marred your lecture I know I'm not a great scholar myself, but I can assure you that I was listening, and I think all of us were listening with great interest to what you were saying As a matter of fact, I've really forgotten what it was now, and that shows how disturbing these interruptions can be. Anyway I know it was something about Sophocles, and what that's got to do with bombing I really fail to see Only a rotten red intellectual would see any connection And may I say, sir, that the way in which he spoke of you, his own father, seems to me absolutely disgusting I happen to know that you are not very much in favour of our Leader (here the young man saluted)," but I should never, think that that was any excuse for me to be lacking in respect or to flout University discipline No doubt your son would call me and my comrades barbarians Let me tell him that we are just ordinary decent people who want nothing better than a quiet life undisturbed by rotten Jews and intellectuals who are always dissatisfied, and so can never be really patriotic As for the troops across the frontier perhaps we'll see whose enemies they are and whose friends. And if it comes to a fight, then perhaps we'll see how some people shape; I mean the people who are always talking about culture and things like that, though all they do about it is to produce a lot of stuff that no decent person can possibly understand Anyway I'm a realist, and I'm not absolutely lacking in good manners either I suppose your son would have started talking about 'the workers' soon if he hadn't had just enough decency to sit down before he came on to that part of his programme The workers! We're all workers, aren't t we? And as for the sort of discontented scum he has in mind, I can tell him that the only thing they're interested in is football pools We'll give them football pools, and we'll give some of their leaders, who are all Jews, something else to think about, too I'm sorry to have been forced to speak, sir, and I vote that now we get back to Sophocles"

The young man sat down and the Professor noted how his hands quivered with the emotion that had prompted his words The latter part of his speech had been interrupted frequently

by exclamations of assent or shouts of protest from the other
students, and by now half a dozen were on their feet The
Professor raised his hand and obtained silence The smile on
his lips as he looked at the angry excited faces showed his wish
to understand and to help rather than any real understanding or
ability to resolve emotional conflicts which, though he admitted
them to be genuine, could not but seem to him somewhat
indecent Or perhaps his smile was just a physical epipheno-
menon, a contraction of muscles as his trained mind in a flash
saw lucidly its own arrangement of facts and arguments, and
was prepared to pursue its subtle and necessary course

"May I," he said, "before we return to the subject of my
lecture, attempt to sum up my impressions of what we have
just heard? First of all, perhaps, I should say that this has
been a somewhat unusual experience for me, and I do not
think that such acrimonious discussion of what, in a very wide
sense, may be called politics is a very good precedent for us to
follow in future But let me say, too, that I respect the genuine
feeling that evidently lay behind both the speeches which we
have heard Indeed, the feeling was so great that it seemed
momentarily to overwhelm all those powers of logical analysis
and arrangement of ideas which are really persuasive and which
I know that both speakers possess May I elaborate this point,
and venture on a word of advice? Emotions spring from such
deep, complicated, and various sources that they must deserve
not only our sympathy but also a most careful examination
The very same emotion—take love, for example—may in
different people or in different circumstances produce quite
divergent courses of action Sometimes the very best and
noblest emotions, inappropriately applied in action, may cause
disaster This lesson is taught by some of our greatest tragedies
A feeling of sympathy for the oppressed, a desire to assure the
greatness and security of one's own country are natural and
worthy feelings May I beg you not to allow these feelings,
which are the more excellent the more strongly they are held,
to divert your attention from the long and difficult process of
reasoning under the guidance of which alone our feelings can
be translated into worthy and satisfactory action? May I
suggest that the fundamental aims of each one of us are not
very different? We all desire peace, security, and justice But
it is by the conscientious use of our reason, not, I think, by any
extravagance of emotion, that those ideals must be realized

Both speakers were actuated by a strong sense of dissatisfaction
with the present state of affairs I share that sense of dissatisfaction But bitter recriminations, whether on one side or on
the other, will not alter facts Let me implore you rather to
examine in the most unprejudiced manner those facts themselves
and the remedies which are proposed Is it, for instance, really
true that the Jews are, whether as an economic or as a racial
organization, a casual element of great importance in our
present discontents? I believe that the best scientific and
economic opinion would lend no support to this view Is
democracy to be condemned outright because in some instances
it has shown itself inefficient? That is hardly, as I think you
will agree, a rational proceeding There was, I imagined, at
the back of the mind of each speaker an assumption that I
found, I confess, most disquietening It was an assumption
that the state (I will avoid the word 'Polis') no longer exists, but
must be, in some way, either reconstituted or purged If this
were true it would be a terrible thing It would mean that there
would be no room withm the framework of the laws for reason
and persuasion to promote the growth towards that ideal state
of affairs which we all seek Do you remember that Socrates,
perhaps the best man who ever lived, voluntarily submitted to
death at the hands of an imperfect government rather than save
his life by breaking the laws which had been established by
consent? I should be the last to maintain that in our state
either material wealth or spiritual liberty is perfectly distributed
I will go further and admit that rational progress is checked by
foices both from without and from within Yet the possibility
of the use of persuasion still remains—free speech, again an
invention of the Greeks"

The Professor paused and noticed that some of the students
had been calmed by his words Their faces wore an expression
almost of gratitude He had not aroused their energy but allayed
their fears Others were unconvinced Among these he
observed a look of bewilderment in his son's eyes, a look of
self-satisfaction, unreasonable in the Professor's view, in the
eyes of the young Legionary

He was about to speak again and, after a few words, to return
to the subject of his lecture when a College messenger, evidently
in haste, entered the hall and, walking quickly between the
tables, came up to the dais and whispered in the Professor's ear
It was the message that now for some days he had been expecting,

yet, although he had expected and prepared for this emergency, the actual delivery of the news caused a sudden loaded feeling at the heart, a rush or withdrawal of blood that would have seemed more appropriate to the reception of some utterly unexpected and very bad news He picked up the copy of Sophocles and placed it beneath his arm

"I regret," he said, "that I shall have to end my lecture at this point, as I am called away by rather urgent business In the meantime I should suggest that you study with particular care (which will be well repaid) the chorus that follows the first episode Finally I would beg you to reflect rather carefully on the general political views I have just put before you If you are inclined to disagree with them, please think as unemotionally as you can of what exactly is your basis for disagreement, of what other general theory you would yourselves put forward, and of whether such a theory would be less or more likely than mine to increase the well-being of mankind"

He went out through the door at the side of the dais and, before he was out of earshot, could hear the raised voices and angry exclamations of the students, an indistinct and unusual sound, behind him While he had been present they had been sufficiently orderly, but the Professor was an honest enough observer to recognize that they had been restrained not by the powers of that persuasion which he had recommended to them, but largely by habit and the respect they had, not for his arguments but for his reputation He recalled an incident which had taken place many years before at a time when he was new to the university He had been walking in the street, and a high wind had blown off a new hat of which he was somewhat proud and which he had scarcely been able to afford The hat had rolled over the pavement to a place where some children were playing, and these children had picked it up and dropped it into the canal. Though he had been, not unnaturally, annoyed at the conduct of these children, he had realized at the time that their action implied no personal affront to himself indeed their feelings towards him might easily have been of the warmest friendship What they had done was rather in the nature of a protest against the restrictions, probably unwise and certainly unsympathetic, with which their lives were surrounded The reasoning faculty, he had realized, does not develop early and requires certain conditions for it to develop at all If he had reasoned with the children then, he would have been speaking beside the point Fear or even habit might have counteracted the urgency of their desire to fling his hat into the canal, reason never The assumptions on which their minds worked were different from those of his own mind

In the case of the students, the problem, he admitted, was more difficult Some, he knew, were still little better than children, easily swayed by any obvious emotional appeal so long as it was directed to some genuine, but unrelated desire that lay near the surface of their minds Such people would be more willing to ascribe their failure in examinations to the Jews than to exert their minds sufficiently to ensure their own success But then there was his son, and many like him A brilliant scholar with an inquiring mind, moreover (and this was the most disquieting fact of all) he shared most of the Professor's own deepest convictions, and yet he had been the most offended by an expression of these convictions in words Was it that the son felt more acutely than the father the urgency of the present situation? It could hardly be that Was the son in greater danger? The reverse was true "I hate because I love" These words were to the Professor the most remarkable that his son had spoken For himself he believed firmly in the maxim that complete understanding would imply complete forgiveness, though not, of course, inactivity Sorrow, disappointment, and disgust he could appreciate, but not hatred Hatred, he admitted, might be aroused in a man by the opposition to his humanity of forces that were merely mechanical or brutal And in human nature there was much brutality, in social organization something mechanical Could such forces ever outweigh love, pity, and understanding? Not, surely, within the framework of a human community, a Polis And this brought the Professor back to his first point Did the community exist? Well he, for one, would fight for its existence

By now he had reached his room where he found waiting for him the messenger from the Chancellor He was requested to call at the Chancellory in an hour's time, and with the reception of this news the Professor felt a sense of relief, not that he desired the responsibility which he knew would be offered him, but because a period of suspense was at an end, an opportunity afforded, even at this eleventh hour, of administering those remedies that, in the Professor's view, should have been applied long ago

In the light of what we know now, it may be easy for some of

us to laugh at this scholar's hopefulness, yet it is difficult to see
how, with the information at his disposal, the Professor could
have realized that his palliatives were about as valuable as
straws He did not know that beyond the frontier the enemy's
plans had been completed three weeks ago He did not suspect
the treachery of the Chief of Police, had only an inkling of the
sums already distributed in bribes and, with his limited knowledge, could not be expected to estimate his own powerlessness.
Indeed, it could hardly be supposed that a man of his character
would have acted differently, nor is it likely that, however he
might have acted, events would have been in any material sense
altered What is perhaps remarkable about the Professor is
that, even supposing him to have possessed at this time the
fullest information, he would not, in all probability, have
departed in any important respect from the course which he
actually pursued

The messenger had gone, and the Professor removed his
gown and began to attire himself for a walk through the streets
to the Chancellory. Before leaving the room he picked up from
a table a silver frame and looked for some moments at the
photograph of a beautiful face, that of Clara, the foreign lady
whom he intended to make his second wife As he looked at the
photograph his thoughts went back to his first wife who had
died when their son had been still a baby He remembered how,
as a young man, he had likened her in his letters to the golden
Helen or, when bathing, to a Nereid Both views, he now
recognized, had been profoundly mistaken She had been a
woman in no way remarkable for intelligence or understanding,
and what had been most important to her had been her womb
Before long the Professor had come to love her as a farmer
might love a favoured cow He thought of her kindly, and
with gratitude, but with little excitement Now, however, his
middle-aged love for Clara had enabled him to regain the
excitement of his youth, and had added to this excitement a
delicious sense of the security that comes from a mutual understanding of life that is beyond the reach of youth Her clothes,
gestures, and the lines of her body were still as fresh to him as
in the days when a girl in a bathing dress would call to his mind
the image of Achilles's mother, what was new to him was the
delight he found in loving her for her ready and sympathetic
mind, her wit, her competent enthusiasm for his own ideals
As he looked at the photographed face that seemed to stare

honestly at him from the paper and not, as is the way of many faces, to swoon sideways or backwards into the frame, he reflected that now he would need Clara's love as never before, and he was grateful to have it She, more than anyone, would rejoice in the opportunity that was soon to be given him, and in her he had at least one informed and unprejudiced adviser. It was characteristic, perhaps, of the good, and certainly of the more lovable qualities of the man that he had no idea whatever of the real situation

CHAPTER II

THE ORATORS

OUTSIDE the College gates the street was almost empty A slow spring breeze swayed a bough covered with white blossom that projected over the pavement from the College gardens One or two of last year's leaves, lately dropped, sidled, with a just perceptible scraping, over the asphalt From a distance, from the factory quarter of the city, the Professor could hear the long-drawn scream of a siren He took his gold watch, a presentation of a foreign university, from his waistcoat pocket and, since the day was already warm, decided to walk to the Chancellory, and on his way to take a turn through the park Exercise for his limbs, sunlight on his skin, the mere sight and proximity of other human beings was what he wanted most, for he had long ago made up his mind about the attitude he would adopt in his coming interview with the Chancellor and, until he knew more exactly what new element in the general situation had caused his summons, he could plan no further in advance

He passed first through the shopping quarter of the town, long, straight streets the pavements of which were already crowded with expensively dressed men and women, whose huge cars hooted melodiously as they manœuvred in the roadway The Professor was surprised to observe that in spite of the economic and political state of the country these crowds were as gay and as large as ever he remembered them to have been He noticed that those shops which retailed such articles as bracelets, lap dogs, and liqueur chocolates seemed to attract the most attention from the passers-by There was one exception, however, to this rule; for in front of a window displaying gas-masks a crowd of smartly-dressed people had completely

blocked the pavement The masks were of different sizes,
shapes, and colours Each style was advertised by a particular
name and the Professor observed on some of the labels beneath
the masks the words "Bulldog," "Sweetheart," "The Tooter,"
"Security," and "The Cosy Nook" The comments of the
crowd were, to the Professor's mind, interesting but inappropriate to the objects on view A young girl, dressed in pink,
exclaimed fastidiously that she could not see herself looking like
a pig A military gentleman was heard to declare that what
was needed was a strong hand on the helm A young man with
a beard pointed out, with some excitement, the similarities
between some of the masks and the work done at a particular
period by a school of negro sculptors But the majority of the
spectators seemed chiefly interested in the ribbons, tassels,
adornments, or patent-fasteners with which the masks were
variously equipped.

At the shop door stood a well-dressed and smiling salesman,
who, as the Professor was passing by, dived into the shop and
emerged again in time to grasp his arm and restrain him from
going "Don't go yet, sir," he said, "I think I have here just the
thing for you, though it was not one of the models displayed
in the window We call it 'The Doctor's Choice Allow me,
sir" And, removing the Professor's hat, he prepared to throw
over his head a large black mask, almost as spacious as a horse's
nose-bag, with the words "Pro Patria" printed in red obliquely
across the upper portion

"Thank you," said the Professor "Not to-day Perhaps
some other time," but he had to employ physical force in order
to disengage himself from the bag and to recover his hat

Even then the young man was not satisfied "Oh come, sir,"
he said "We must all be prepared, mustn't we? It won't be
long now, you know"

The Professor was still somewhat nettled. "What won't be
long now?" he asked rather sharply

"Why, the war!" replied the salesman, still smiling, and
added, "Patriotism, you know, sir I think so anyway"

The Professor looked at him keenly Was this young man,
he wondered, able at all clearly to imagine how he would appear
if half his face were blown away? Had he a notion of the
extremes of pain or of the disgust which is usually aroused by
the sight of ulcers or of maggots in open wounds? Yes, he
must have, and yet for some reason his imagination was in-

operative Was it that the nature of his job required that this faculty should not be employed, demanded instead an expression of semi-idiocy, an overweening confidence that no sane person could possibly feel?

Just then the proprietor of the shop joined the group outside his window He was a middle sized man with closely-cropped hair He looked, and was proud to look, a perfect, though undistinguished gentleman Alone of those in the crowd he had recognized the Professor, and he greeted him with a slight but grave inclination of the head "Good morning, Professor," he said "I hope that my assistant has not been tioubling you" The young salesman looked nervously at his employer He had failed, evidently, to recognize that he had been addressing a person of importance Smiling more than ever he retreated hurriedly into the shop The shopkeeper took no further notice of him With his head slightly on one side, and his hand on his hip he began to speak in a cultured voice and a severely judicial manner "I hope that our display affects you favourably, Professor," he said "I think I may say that at least it is artistic. But I am sorry to say that many of our clients fail to realize that, quite apart from the colour scheme and the lines of our models, these masks have another great advantage I can assure you that they really are remarkably efficient Rather different, I believe, sir, from the masks supplied by the Government."

"How is that?" the Professor asked "I had always been under the impression that all masks were made to a general pattern approved by the Government, and that the best available talent was applied in the Government's service"

The shopkeeper smiled "Oh no, Professor," he said, "that is, I think, hardly the postion We, for instance, employ a staff of scientists, who, I think I may say, are doing work that is rather superior to anything done in the Government departments They get higher salaries, you see"

"I suppose then," said the Professor, "that you are in close touch with the Government department If your scientists can co-operate with the Government you will be doing a great service to the nation"

The shopkeeper looked gravely at the Professor He seemed eager to explain "Ideally speaking, sir," he said, "ideally speaking that would be all very well Service, after all, is our motto" And he pointed to an inscription to that effect which adorned the wall above the shop window "But I am afraid that if we were to adopt your suggestion, we should soon be driven out of business It is rather a question, is it not, sir, of paying the piper? But though our productions can unfortunately not be made available to everyone we can at least say that we are making sure that the important people, people like yourself, sir, are receiving the very best articles"

"You mean the richer people," said the Professor abruptly. "I am afraid that I cannot agree with you that these are necessarily the most important" He observed a look of some consternation in the shopkeeper's eyes and hastened to add, "But you may be sure that I appreciate your difficulties It is a matter to which the Government should attend at once; indeed an intolerable situation"

If the Professor had hoped that his words would have any reassuring effect on the shopkeeper he was disappointed There was a look almost of hatred in the man's eyes as he answered in a smooth voice, "I think, sir, that we can get on quite well without Government interference"

The Professor recovered quickly from the shock of the man's evidently changed attitude "It is rather a question," he said, "of whether the Government, and the people, can get on without interfering Good morning, sir," and he walked on hurriedly, forcing his way through the crowds that still stood staring at the gas-masks, and then proceeded more sedately, stepping now and then into the gutter to give way to a lady or a lady's dog

He found it difficult for some moments to rid his mind of the feeling of irritation that had been aroused by the conduct of the salesman and the shopkeeper It was on such people that, in the city, the Government depended, and yet neither of the two seemed to have the slightest idea that the situation was almost desperate The Professor consoled himself with the reflection that the instincts of the people were sound, but at the back of his mind he was still aware that instincts unrelated to any rational view of living are unreliable and thus dangerous His thoughts went back to the interruption of his lecture. His son, at all events, could imagine the extent of the danger to which the shopkeeper and his assistant had seemed quite indifferent And yet his son, like them, was in opposition to the Government, had declared openly that the community did not exist Where was his support? Who were the men of good will?

He had now reached the park and, inside the gates, paused

to let his eyes wander over the chestnut trees, already showing green, the long expanse of grass dotted with strolling figures and, nearer to him, the stands of public speakers and the smaller or larger crowds with which they were surrounded All his life he had been in the habit of listening, whenever he passed that way, to the speakers in the park, although he had seldom received from them any information which was not either false or already known to him And yet he had been at all times delighted in watching the give and take of argument or invective that could be often observed at these meetings, and he had felt proud of his country as being one of the few in which citizens in a public place were allowed to advocate openly almost any doctrme Nothing but good, he had felt, could come of the open discussion even of such views as that the world was flat, or that a panacea to the evils of the world could be found in a slight alteration of the currency He had been less pleased with what had lately become so common, the huge demonstrations either of the National Legion or of the Reds, for at these meetings he had noticed that logical argument was not often attempted and that the speakers served rather to reinforce the effects of bands and banners than to present a clear description of the views they maintained Yet the Professor would argue stubbornly against anyone who proposed a ban on such demonstrations The only interference which he would support would be a regulation by which no party should be allowed to spend more money on propaganda than any other party

There would be, of course, no big demonstration organized for this hour of the day The Professor began to walk slowly towards one of the stands which seemed to have attracted the attention of quite a crowd of people and, approaching more closely, read on a placard the words "Miss de Lune The International Progressive Nudist Association Peace and Purity" The audience consisted largely of unemployed men and women, whose haggard faces, cheap and insufficient clothing would be, thought the Professor, in themselves enough evidence to show to what a state of poverty and insecurity the country had been reduced

Miss de Lune's own followers who were arrayed in two bands, sexually segregated, on the right and left of the platform, made an imposing show The women were dressed in sandals, shorts, and brassieres, and the men were similarly attired except that they lacked what many of them seemed to need, the brassieres The partially exposed bodies, thought the Professor, were at least well fed, but in this respect Miss de Lune herself outdid any of her followers She was a monstrous woman, largely crab-coloured, with, a voice like a bull Standing by her on the platform was a tall man dressed in a turban and loin cloth, quite motionless and seeming indifferent to the flood of words which Miss de Lune was pouring round him

"He is my Guru," she was roaring as the Professor joined the crowd "He first taught me the lesson of Liberation He first taught me that I am a moving shadow"

Here there was an interruption "How much does that weigh?" someone had shouted from the back of the crowd, but the nudists turned like one man on the heckler and a thin-shanked youth pronounced in a piping voice the words "Oh, you cad"

The Professor himself would have anticipated further inter-ruptions, and it was almost with a feeling of dismay that he looked at the crowd whose tired eyes and sullen faces showed them to be too apathetic even to comment on the fervent oratory which, for all their concern, might have been addressed to the moon A squadron of aeroplanes was frying across the sky over their heads Some members of the audience, their attention attracted by the swelling drone, looked upwards but, if they thought anything, there was no expression of thought in their faces The big bodies of the bombers passed behind the trees

Miss de Lune continued, still shouting "My friends, we are living in the Kali-Yug Let me repeat it We are living in the Kali-Yug" Here the sympathetic portion of her audience, the nudists themselves, wobbled like jellies Miss de Lune breathed in heavily and proceeded "The Kali-Yug, my friends, is as, you know, the fourth age of world-manifestation, the Black Age, and we are in it What do we see everywhere? Strikes, unemployment, wars, licentiousness of all kinds What are these but signs, which no one can deny, of the Kali-Yug? Oh, my friends, how can we escape?" There was a hush, expressive of uncertainty, before the speaker continued. "I will tell you, my friends, I will repeat the lesson which I have learnt from my Guru" Here the man in the turban appeared suddenly to recover consciousness and surprised the Professor by dipping a quick bow before returning to his state of immobility "Oh friends," Miss de Lune continued to shout," let us enter into awareness of the perfection from which when perfection is subtracted it is still perfection How simple it all is! We do not exist This does not exist"(here she slapped herself powerfully on both haunches)"I do not exist You do not exist I am not I. I am a part of the Great I And not a part I am a shadow I am a dream It is so refreshing, my friends It is so, so refreshing And it is on this great principle, my friends, that the great body, or rather great soul of International Progressive Nudism is based Away with trappings! Let us bare our bodies, so far as a reactionary police will allow, to the stars, and we shall forget them For the body is not a body, my friends You will make, I assure you, a great mistake if you think that. It is a vehicle, or rather the shadow of a vehicle To be exact my friends, it is the shadow of a vehicle for a shadow Let us not, then, treat it as if it were a real thing, loading it with costly silks, protecting it with, for example, an umbrella Let us gambol in the sun and forget it Let us lay it every night in a position at right angles to the equator, so that the cosmic rays may draw us into the plane of unreality that is super-reality, out of the Kali-Yug, my friends, into the unmatenabihty, my dear friends, of insubstantialness "insubstantialness

The Professor was astounded For a moment he thought of intervening Should he cry out, "Ladies and Gentlemen, how can such words be addressed to men and women who have not enough to eat?" Or should he strike at the intellectual foundations of the creed? "One need not be," he might say, "very conversant with Hindu philosophy to be quite sure that the names Krta-Yug, Trita-Yug, Dvapara-Yug, and Kah-Yug (four names derived from the numbers of dots on dice and which may be held to correspond with the Golden, Silver, Bronze, and Iron Ages of European mythology)—one may be sure, I say, that these names can have very little reference to the world in which we live to-day" Should he demand evidence for the alleged effect of cosmic rays on a body lying at right angles to the equator? He would do nothing of all this, for what most perplexed him was the reflection that while a voice was speaking and while ears were listening, there seemed to be no relation between the two, and he himself, except as a mere spectator, was unrelated with either He was accustomed, however, rather to smile at folly than to condemn it, and even now, inappropriate as any show of mirth might seem to the present situation, he was, perhaps almost automatically, smiling at the nudists and their vociferous leader.

Words spoken at his side startled him "I can't see anything to laugh at" He looked round and saw an old man, dressed in black, shabbily, whose thin, peaked face was chiefly remarkable for its deep-set black eyes which, being concentrated on the Professor, seemed to denote a kind of accusation in which there was some element of despair Strangely there came into the Professor's head words which were perhaps suggested by what his son Had said at the lecture, "I laugh because I love," but he did not speak these words "I agree with you, sir," he said "This is certainly not the time for such nonsense"

The old man continued his steady stare "I very much doubt," he said, "whether you agree with me at all. I know who you are, Professor"

The Professor looked more closely at the old man's face It was intent, but not angry "Perhaps," said the Professor, "you belong to one of the extreme parties"

"And you," replied the old man, "belong to no party at all No doubt you imagine that you will, because you have a reputation for honesty, succeed in forming such a thing as a united movement of people whom perhaps you think of as 'men of good will' Have you any idea who these people are apart from a few university lecturers, some doctors, and school teachers, whose ability in street fighting is, to say the least, unproved?"

The Professor was surprised but not offended by this outspoken criticism Indeed, there was something in the old man's face, an expression of energy reminding him more of youth than age, which rather attracted him "I think," he said, "that you are attributing to me a vaguer policy than any that I should be likely to put forward What would you say if I were, from a stiictly non-party basis, to put before the people almost the whole economic programme of the Left together with a plea for national unity in the face of the foreign danger?"

The old man looked up at him sharply "I should pity you from the bottom of my heart," he said, and was about to say something more when they were assailed by a rich tenor voice: "I say, half a mo, you chaps"

The Professor looked in the direction of the voice. He saw a platform placarded with the words, "The Rev Furius Webber. The Peace-through-Spinning Movement," It was the Rev.

Furius himself who had addressed them, no doubt wishing to make an addition to his somewhat sparse audience Though, if there were few listeners on the grass below the platform, there there were plenty of supporters at the clergyman's side on the platform itself The Professor had heard of the Peace-through-Spinmng Movement and knew that it was an organization almost entirely confined to the very rich, with a sprinkling of young schoolmasters and their wives Women with diamonds and young men, red-faced and wearing golfing clothes now stood smiling at the Rev Webber's side The clergyman himself was tall, dark, and handsome, a young man who, it was said, would go far in the Church, one who was particularly notable for his "man-to-man approach" and for what his admirers described as his sincerity He was now leaning forward fiom the platform and addressing himself to the Professor

"It's awfully decent of you, sir," he was saying, "to stop and join us I'm not going to make a long speech, because I think that would be an awful bore As a matter of fact, I'm only he e to introduce to you our chairman, the distinguished scientist and explorer, Dr Cornelius Chough," and so saying he gently pushed to the front of the platform a small and undistinguished looking old gentleman who seemed oblivious of his audience, but was scanning intently through rather thick spectacles a piece of paper which he held in his hand After turning this paper over and over and examining it from all angles, as though he had been struck by a thought of the possibility of reading his speech backwards or from right to left across the page, Dr. Chough announced his readiness to proceed by making a loud and unexpected trumpeting noise, then began to speak in a voice the monotony of which was relieved by an undertone of perplexity occasioned by the difficulty he found in reading his own writing

"Hrumph! Hrumph! No one," he said, "can contemplate the outbreak of a conflagration without a feeling that is akin, without a feeling that is akin, that is akin, that is akin to dis— without a feeling that is akin to dis—, Hrumph! Hrumph! to dismay"

"Hear, hear!" said the Rev Furius Webber in his suavest manner, but his chairman took no notice of him at all

"I am here to-day," he continued, with his face bent over the piece of paper, "for one reason only, and that is to give service to a great Hrumph! a great Ideal. There is a widespread need at the present time for Hrumph! Hrumph! Hrumph! I say that there is a demand to-day for" Here the doctor must have been compelled to omit a passage from his speech, for he continued, "Raffia work Hrumph! We do a lot of it, in addition to tablecloths, footstools, bedspreads I am asked to say that the proceeds of these activities are devoted in all cases to Hrumph! to a fund for our Hrumph! Hrumph! for our propaganda in favour of a round table conference on economic collaboration And now I have an announcement to make We have a little girl Hrumph! Hrumph! We have a little girl who"

Dr Chough had come to the end of the writing on the paper and now he turned, in no way disconcerted by what might have seemed an unsatisfactory display, to the Rev Webber The clergyman stepped briskly forward, and Dr Chough merged inconspicuously with the other supporters who thronged the platform "We are lucky enough," said the Rev Furius Webber, "as our Chairman has pointed out, to have with us to-day a little girl who can recite a poem by William Blake. You've only got to read one or two of his things, by the way, to see that he was a pacifist all right Anyway the poem that little Fleur is going to recite is called 'Jerusalem' and I can promise you all a treat even if some of you have read this poem before But first of all, just to get us into the right mood, I vote that we have three jolly good cheers for peace Come on now, chaps! All together Hip, Hip, Hip, Hurray!"

The cheers were given musically by the rich women and somewhat hoarsely by the schoolmasters The Professor looked to his side for the old man who had stopped him to listen to the pacifists Had this old man, he wondered, maliciously or by accident conducted him to a meeting where a non-party view was to be expressed? He would have liked to explain more clearly to this sceptic the precise details of his own plan for national co-operation, but, to his surprise, the old man had gone

The Professor looked again at his watch and, neglecting the recitation, began to walk more quickly across the Park Though the air was refreshing and the sunlight warm, his mind had been by no means lightened as a result of the conversations and speeches which he had heard that morning He was inclined now to wish that he had spent the time of waiting for his interview either with Clara, who would have given him sympathy, or with his son who, however much he might object to the use of the word "Polis," would at least have had something to say which was not entirely irrelevant. With the old man, too, he would have liked to have had further talk, for the old man had seemed to express some sympathy with his intentions and a complete lack of faith in his ability to make them real

The Professor, still walking, put his stick under his arm and spread out his hands in an appealing gesture to nothing in particular He was attempting, in imagination, to convince his critics. "Surely, gentlemen, there is such a thing as justice? Surely a temporary programme, demonstrably just, voted on and not imposed, can serve as a rallying point for the citizens of a country that is in danger of invasion?" He became aware, from the amused glances of the passers-by, that he was acting somewhat oddly and, quickening his step, he reached the further side of the Park and turned into the street which led to the Chancellory

Here quite a large crowd had collected and the Professor found that he had to walk between a police cordon and remove his hat from time to time in acknowledgment of the cheers with which he was greeted Evidently a rumour of the changed situation in the Government had already reached the public, and the Professor was glad to find some confirmation of his hopes in the sight of the applauding crowds, few of whom, he imagined, could know much either of him personally or of his work, but who Seemed for the most part to consist of his well-wishers

He had reached the steps of the Chancellory and had turned for the last time before mounting them to salute the crowd when he saw a figure dart through the police cordon and run towards him across the road It was the old man with whom he had talked in the Park, and the Professor was for the moment more surprised than alarmed to observe that he was holding a revolver in his hand as he approached He reached the Professor before the police could overtake him, and the Professor, dropping his walking-stick, seized the outstretched arm of his assailant and by twisting his wrist forced him to let the weapon fall on to the pavement

Two police officers, red-faced and indignant, grasped the old man from behind and jerked him off his feet, and then one of them, turning to the Professor, said "Remarkably smart work sir Great presence of mind, if you don't mind me saying so'

The crowd, after a moment's hush, had begun to shout angrily and to surge forward against the cordon of police in an effort to get at the old man who was now standing upright, making no effort to escape, and looking, thought the Professor, on the whole rather pleased with himself than frightened or disappointed The whole affair had taken place so quickly and had caused him so little difficulty or discomfort that the Professor himself could hardly believe that he had been in any danger But now a portion of the crowd had broken through the police Shouting, some with raised umbrellas, some with crooked fingers, they were evidently set on lynching the prisoner. The Professor motioned to the two policemen to take the old man into the Chancellory He himself raised his hand and began to speak The crowd's attention was diverted and their excitement gradually subsided

"My friends," said the Professor, "I thank you for the concern which you have shown for my safety I am quite uninjured I beg you not to attach too much importance to this clumsy attempt on my life It is the work, I am sure, not of a political opponent, but of some poor Creature who will be found, I expect, to be of an unbalanced mind In any case it is not our function to judge him, and still less to punish him He will be tried in accordance with the law and it is our duty in all things to abide by the law Thank you once more, my friends, for the confidence in me which you have expressed by your applause and by your concern for me I shall do all I can to deserve that confidence"

By now the prisoner was safe behind the doors of the Chancellory The expressions on the faces of the crowd, and their gestures, were less threatening "Three cheers for the Professor!" someone shouted, and at the end of this impressive and apparently sincere ovation the Professor himself entered the house and found the prisoner and the two policemen chatting inside the doorway The two policemen sprang to attention when they saw him and once more grasped the arms of the unresisting old man

"If you please," said the Professor, "I should like to have a word alone with your prisoner, before you take him away. But see first of all that he is unarmed."

"Certainly, sir," said the senior of the two officers. "But are you sure that it would be wise, if you will allow me to say so?"

"I think that I am quite capable of holding my own," said the Professor, "if it should come to a tussle But if you like you may remain outside the door and I will call for you should I require your help"

The officer saluted and, having emptied the old man's pockets and patted him about the body, he led the way into an unoccupied room and, with a nod that seemed almost conspiratorial, retired

"Sit down," said the Professor, and looked hard at the old man's face which bore no trace of fear or, which was more odd, of any kind of nervous reaction which, so the Professor thought, might be expected to result from the failure of his attempt at murder and from his arrest "I should like you to explain to me," he said, "why exactly you wished just then to assassinate me And I am also puzzled by the fact that you chose such an unfavourable moment to make your attack You could have done the same thing much more easily and safely while we were together in the Park"

The old man first glanced towards the door and then leant forward across the table at which he was sitting "I had hoped," he said, "that you would notice that and would perhaps give me an opportunity to speak Not that I'm in any danger myself I'm a detective, you see. The whole affair was a put-up job."

The Professor had at first not really believed that the old man was mentally unbalanced Now, however, he smiled at him compassionately "I see," he said "You mean that you are working in collaboration with the police?"

"Yes, certainly," the old man replied, and then observing that the Professor was not taking him seriously, a remarkably gay smile came for a second to his haggard face "Forgive me, Professor," he said "I admit that what I say sounds incredible But will you, when the Chief of Police talks to you about this, tell him that you recognized that the man who attacked you was Sergeant Jinkerman See what he says then But in case he should decide to go on bluffing, please listen to what is in fact, the truth"

The old man was speaking so calmly and showed so obvious an appreciation of what was going on in the Professor's mind, that it was impossible to consider him as insane The Professor listened carefully as he continued "No doubt," he was saying, "you thought that the people who were applauding you in the streets were genuine supporters of your policy Perhaps some of them were But the greater part of the demonstration was organized by the Chief of Police An account of it and of the attempt on your life will by this time have reached the newspapers It will be suggested that the attack was the work of the Reds, and there will be a demand that their meetings and their papers should be at once suppressed You see the idea? The plan was to strengthen your hand"

The Professor stared in amazement at the old man's pale face with its tragic eyes "So far from that being the case," he said, "the plan, if I can believe your story, seems to have been to force my hand But if your story is true why are you telling it to me? You cannot imagine that I would look with sympathy on such a piece of falsehood You must know that, if I believed your story, I should refuse to countenance the suppression of the Reds, and would be more likely to demand the resignation of the Chief of Police, and perhaps your own dismissal"

"Exactly," said the old man "And, if you will proceed a little further in your reasoning, you will see that I could not have told you my story if I had not myself been sympathetic to the Reds To tell the truth I occupy a rather important position in their organization You must not think that I am not your enemy. But I realize that your devotion to abstract justice—what I regard as your fatal weakness—will, in this instance, be of service to the concrete justice of my cause"

The Professor smiled "At some other time," he said, "I should be glad to exchange views with you about the relation between abstract and conciete justice At the moment I can assure you that what you call my weakness will be used, if I can verify your story, to increase your strength May I, however, before I leave you suggest that if not our methods at least our aims are very similar?"

He got up from his chair His mind was filled with a deep feeling of sympathy with the old man who, if his story was correct, must have passed many years of danger and insecurity in the police force which, as even the Professor was, prepared to admit, was more hostile than impartial to the organization to which he said he belonged The Professor held out his hand and the old man shook it as though he were undertaking yet anothei unpleasant duty "You are talking like a speaker in the Park," he said

Chapter III

THE EXECUTIVE

By the time that the Professor had reached the door of the room where the Cabinet was meeting he was some four or five minutes late for his appointment, and when he opened the door he observed signs of impatience or of suppressed excitement in those he would soon have as his colleagues Dr Tromp, the Chancellor, was sitting dejectedly at the head of the long polished table, holding a watch in his hand He was a small undistinguished-looking man, who many years ago had made a name for himself as a physicist, and afterwards, for reasons which would be difficult to explain, had become leader of the Agrarian Party He bitterly resented the accusations of weakness and incompetence which had been made against his Government, but was not sorry now to be relinquishing power. Next to him, and also seated at the table, was the representative of the Orthodox Trade Union Federation, a big man with a h ead that was still big in proportion to his body He was noted for the extreme violence of his public utterances and his extreme pliability in any private discussion Now he was drumming on the table with his rather thick fingers His lips were pursed together as though he were about to whistle a tune.

Colonel Grimm, the Chief of Police, was standing with his back to the window and with his hands in his pockets His appearance was in strange contrast with his name, for he was a little, dapper man, looking scarcely older than thirty, and the beginnings of a smile, which might have betokened amusement or might be merely a trick of the nerves, were constantly appearing at the corners of his thin mouth The other member of the Cabinet who was present was the Minister for War, a very old man, partially deaf, who was called by his colleagues "The Commodore" although it was known that he had never held any naval or military rank He was leaning back in an armchair with half-closed eyes when the Professor entered the room and was saying, in a somewhat thick voice, "There is one factor in the situation which dominates all the others"— words to which no one was paying the slightest attention

Before the Professor had had tune to close the door behind him Colonel Grimm had crossed the room towards him and was greeting him with outstretched hand. "May I be the first," he said, "to congratulate you, Professor, on your remarkable escape? I should like, too, to compliment you on the daring which you showed It was an example to us all"

There was a chorus of approbation from the other members of the Cabinet The Professor observed Colonel Grimm's curious habit of giving two complete and successive smiles at the conclusion of his sentences It was as though the muscles of his mouth were operated by a kind of mechanism such as that which is attached to some cameras He looked steadily at the man's eyes "I had imagined," he said, "that in my assailant I had recognized Detective-Sergeant Jinkerman"

For a moment the Colonel's face preserved an expression of uncertainty, then his smiles came in quick succession "My dear Professor," he said, "you are much too clever for us I hope, however, that you realized the advantage of the little deception which I am afraid that I attempted to practise It will greatly increase your popularity, and it will put you in a very strong position should it be necessary for you to take any emergency measures to deal with the present rather alarming situation"

The Trade Union leader banged his fist on the table. "Do you mean to tell me," he shouted, "that the whole thing was a hoax?"

The retiring Chancellor leant towards him and said in a voice that expressed some deference, "Exactly, my dear fellow. Equivocal, you know Equivocal"

The Trade Union leader nodded his head slowly, and pursed his lips "Ah," he said, "that's just what I say"

The Professoi had turned to the Chancellor "May I assume," he said, "that you have called me here this morning to make me the offer which you made unofficially last night?"

The Chancellor inclined his head in a motion that seemed to express dejection as well as assent

The Professor did not wait for him to sepak "In that case," he said, "may I deal with this business at once?" He turned quickly to the Chief of Police whose smiling face assumed an expression of humiliation when he met the Professor's eye. "I can scarcely find words," the Professor began—and indeed the agitation with which he spoke was unusual to him—"I can scarcely find words to express my abhorrence from any deliberate falsifying of the facts which are put before the public That this falsification was organized not by an irresponsible newspaper man, but by a Government official makes the thing a hundred times worse I have half a mind, sir, to demand your resignation One thing I certainly do demand, and that is that any plans which you may have made for reporting this event in the press should be immediately cancelled"

The vigour with which the Professor had expressed himself had evidently come as a shock to his colleagues They sat still with varying expressions of surprise on their faces, all except the Commodore, who now leant forward in his chair and, holding his hand to his ear, said in a rather gruff voice, "I beg your pardon I did not quite catch the last remark"

The Chancellor came nimbly to his side and whispered in his other ear words which were audible to everyone else in the room, "Never mind, my dear fellow, never mind We'll tell you afterwards"

"What?" said the Commodore, "I can't hear a thing on that side of my head Thought you knew that Deaf as a post" The Chancellor repeated his remark, this time from the other side of the chair, and the Commodore nodded his head as though some secret had been imparted to him He sat bolt upright and stared in consternation at the Chief of Police who was now on his knees before the Professor

"I beg you to believe," he was saying, "that what I did I did only with the interests of the nation and the Government at heart. I appreciate to the full the moral objections which may be made to what I have done In fact I am convinced now, my dear sir, that I was mistaken And if you should demand my resignation I shall loyally place it in your hands May I say, however, that at the present moment a reorganization of the Police Force might have rather dangerous consequences? I entreat you, sir, to allow me under your authority to continue to serve my country"

The Professor was not mollified, but he realized that a split in the Police Force at such a time would indeed be dangerous, and he was actually willing to believe that Colonel Grimm's conduct, dishonourable as it was, had yet been prompted by a kind of patriotism With a gesture of his hand he invited the Chief of Police to rise from his suppliant position "What about the newspapers?" he said "Will it be possible to prevent them from commenting on this incident?"

"I am afraid, Sir," said the Chief of Police, "that all the papers will by this time have received an account of what has

happened But I can, if you wish, arrange that they point out
the attack was not the work of any political organization, but
of a lunatic"

The Professor turned towards the other members of the
Cabinet "You see, gentlemen," he said, "how falsehood
breeds falsehood" He spoke sadly for, though he was by no
means superstitious, it appeared to him that there was something most unpleasing, even inauspicious, in the fact that his
first exercise in authority should be to countenance the broadcasting of a lie

The retiring Chancellor addressed him with a certain diffidence "My dear Professor," he said "Do not believe for a
moment that I do not share your scruples But since this
unfortunate affair has happened, might it not be, in the interests
of the nation, of course, from some points of view anyway,
desirable at least in some way or other to make some use of
what has occurred? We might, for example, use the incident
in order not to suppress, but in some measure to confine the
activities of at least one of the extreme parties I can assure
you that in my view—and I think the majority of our colleagues
will agree with me—such a step would be highly beneficial The
means we might adopt, should you, my dear sir, approve,
might not be in the most precise sense of the word honest,
but the end, my dear sir! The end is not merely honest, it is
positively worth while By means of a small deception we
might save the state"

"I am entirely in agreement," shouted the Commodore, who
was still sitting as upright as a rod of metal on the edge of his
chair, "although I am afraid that I did not quite catch the last
sentence."

The representative of the Orthodox Trade Unions had risen
to his feet "No one in this room," he said in a threatening
tone, "will call me an extremist I am against a dictatorship
whether from the Left or from the Right" He sat down again
and, with his head lowered like a bull, looked from side to side
fiercely at his colleagues, who were quite unable to see in what
sense his declaration of faith was meant to be applied to the
point at issue

The Professor looked straight at Dr Tromp It had not
been, he imagined, without the assent of the Chancellor that
the Chief of Police had in the first place ai ranged for the sham
assassination He spoke sharply, and behind his spectacles his

eyes were blinking rapidly "Dr Tromp, if you still wish me to take on the duties of Chancellor, I must insist that there be no further discussion on this point Even had a real attempt on my life been made I should never think of that as an excuse for depriving any citizen of his constitutional rights On this matter, gentlemen, my mind is made up If you wish for my services in the Government you must allow Colonel Grimm to leave the room at once and to make the best and most decent arrangements he can with the newspapers, though nothing he can say will be, I am afraid, exactly true"

The Chancellor's acquiescence seemed to the Professor more like despair He nodded his head wearily and the Chief of Police left the room, saluting the Professor before leaving. The Commodore subsided into the comfort of his chaii, and the representative of the Trade Unions pronounced a sentence of which the words "undemocratic decision" were alone audible.

The Chancellor took off his glasses and wiped them with his handkerchief He then passed his hand in a sawing motion several times across the nape of his neck and immediately, as though this exercise had suddenly restored his energy, began to speak "My dear sir," he said, "I can only hope that you will not regret this step when I inform you of what has happened this morning We have been given what I am really almost inclined to describe as an ultimatum"

"Of an undemocratic nature," interrupted the Trade Union leader in an injured tone of voice

The Professor had taken a seat at the table and was watching the Chancellor closely "You mean from across the frontier?" he said

"Precisely," replied the Chancellor, and his thin lips quivered, though whether in fear or in indignation it was impossible to say "The Ambassador was with me this morning There was nothing in writing, you understand But he hinted—indeed I may go further and say that he actually mentioned the use of armed force"

The Commodore demonstratively cleared his throat. He spoke pompously in the direction of the Professor "And that, sir," he said, "is in my view a factor in the situation which outweighs everything else"

The Professor nodded his assent before turning again to the Chancellor "And what are the conditions," he asked, "which the Ambassador mentioned?"

Once more the Chancellor began to saw the nape of his neck

with the back of his hand "Very difficult," he said, "very
difficult indeed for me to specify I may say that the Ambassador began by informing me that his Government regarded us
as incapable of preserving order within our own boundaries
Gentlemen, I need hardly tell you that I found that exasperat-
ing" He paused and, in order to conceal his emotion, blew
his nose with a surprisingly loud trumpeting noise

The Professor's face was very grim "Insolence'" he
muttered, for his mind had gone back to earlier periods of
history, when small and united states had often fought their
oppressors and had, not infrequently, either gained or retained
their independence

The Chancellor had now taken off his spectacles Without
them he appeared, as the Professor could not help noticing,
both frightened and bewildered "I expressed myself with
some force," he said in a timid voice "I told the Ambassador
that we could not tolerate any interference I informed him
that we were in complete control of the situation Gentlemen,
at this point I can only describe the Ambassador's attitude as
failing in respect"

The Commodore, behaving somewhat in the manner of a
jack-in-the-box, again stiffened his spine and began to address
the company at large in a slow voice "It's a damned queer
thing that, because many years ago now, when I was on a
shooting holiday over there, I remember saying quite often to
my wife—that, of course, would be my first wife—I remember
saying to her that those fellows had no manners at all Never
have had One mustn't expect it."

At this point in the Commodore's reminiscences the Chief
of Police returned to the room "I think I have settled that
matter satisfactorily," he whispered to the Professor before
taking his seat at the table "We were just hearing," said the
Professor, "of what the Chancellor describes as an ultimatum
Please continue, Dr Tromp"

The Chancellor sat back in his chair and spread out his
hands, palms upward, on the table He made no effort to
disguise his emotion As he spoke, his voice often died away
into a note of despair, and tears of vexation appeared at the
corners of his eyes "What could I do, gentlemen?" he said
"The Ambassador showed a complete lack of respect. When
I remonstrated with him he went so far as to comment on my
personal appearance He asserted that his Government could

occupy this country in twenty-four hours, and actually stated that our fellow-countrymen would welcome the invasion Gentlemen, I may say that I was, in a manner of speaking, almost browbeaten. The Ambassador demanded (I think I am justified in using that word) a change of Government, and under the circumstances I was in a way rather relieved to be able to tell him that the Government actually would be changed or at least reconstituted. I mentioned your name, Professor, and I am afraid that the Ambassador did not appear altogether pleased to hear it. Nevertheless we are unanimous in wishing you to accept the Chancellorship, and I may say that I hope that you will be more successful in this difficult position than I have been."

The Chancellor appeared to be on the point of bursting into tears, but was surprisingly heartened when the Professor rose from his chair and warmly shook his hand "I accept the responsibility, gentlemen," said the Professor, "on the understanding that, when you have seen my programme, you will give me your full support But may I ask first of all whether the Ambassador made any other demands to you except for a change in the Government?"

The ex-Chancellor, now that he had relinquished his power, was much more cheerful He began to polish his spectacles vigorously and spoke brightly, almost as though he had something amusing to say "Nothing out of the common," he said "The Ambassador made the familiar remarks about the question of the minorities He also said that relations between his Government and ours could never improve until we had repressed the Red Trade Unions"

The representative of the Orthodox Unions interrupted in a fierce voice "And what did he have the face to say about our Unions, I should like to know?"

Dr Tromp was momentarily startled "Oh, nothing, my dear fellow," he replied "Absolutely nothing, I assure you. He only said that if there was a Trade Union representative in the Government, there should also be a representative of the National Legion But his animadversions, my dear sir, were confined to the Red Unions"

"May I explain to you, gentlemen," said the Professor, "some of the reasons why this conduct of the Ambassador appears to me so insolent? Not only is it a disgraceful thing that our policy should be dictated to us from outside, but what is more disgraceful is the fact that the policy recommended to us is demonstrably unjust Take the case of this demand, that the National Legion should be represented in the Government Recent elections have shown clearly that the Legion can only count on a small minority of votes Actually the largest organized bodies in the state are the Trade Unions. The Orthodox Unions and the Red Unions, together must account for nearly 70 per cent, of the male electorate It is known that this 70 per cent is bitterly opposed to the policy of the Legion Consequently, although we shall always be glad to listen to deputations from any minority, to appoint a member of the Legion to a post in the Government would be to act contrary to the interests of democracy"

The Professor paused since he had caught the eye of the representative of the Orthodox Unions who now, very red in the face, began to speak. "I protest," he said "I protest in the strongest possible terms against any suggestion that the Orthodox Unions are in any way allied with the Reds"

"I was merely suggesting," said the Professor with a smile, "that both organizations are opposed on much the same grounds to the policy of the Legion And you will agree with me, no doubt, that both organizations have certain immediate aims in common, such aims, I mean, as the conservation and possible extension of the rights of collective bargaining, workers' control in industry and so on"

"That is not the point at all," said the Orthodox leader more fiercely than ever "The point is that I am opposed to a dictatorship whether from the Right or from the Left"

The Professor endeavoured to conceal the impatience which he felt "I can assure you," he said, "that I have no intention of introducing a dictatorship I am merely trying to estimate the real and effective will of the people whom we represent The policy which I am going to recommend to you is based on two assumptions first that there is a majority of peihaps 90 per cent of the people in favour of retaining our country's national integrity and independence, second, that there is a smaller, but definite majority in favour of a change in the economic system along the general lines advocated not only by the Trade Unions but by many economists, scientists and political theorists who are not members of those Unions I propose first of all to hold at the earliest possible moment a plebiscite in which the electorate will be asked the simple question, 'Are you in favour of this country retaining its complete political independence?' The result of this plebiscite should be to stiffen the morale of our own countrymen and greatly to strengthen our position abroad My next step will be to put forward in the name of the Government a programme for social and economic reform, and I beg you, gentlemen, to look favourably on this programme It will be described by its critics as a socialist programme Personally I should prefer to call it a programme of efficiency and justice. Each point in the programme has been discussed and rediscussed by experts I can assure you that there is no doubt whatever not only that the programme will work, but that it will be a vast improvement from the point of view of mere efficiency, on our present system But, gentlemen, there is another point to which I attach the very greatest importance. We shall be, I believe, even in this small country, an inspiration to the rest of mankind if we can bring about by democratic means what amounts to a social and economic revolution I have no doubt whatever in my own mind that the changes which I shall recommend are socially just and economically necessary, also that a majority of our fellow-countrymen will be found to be in favour of my programme Were this programme to be carried through, gentlemen, as the result of a free vote of the people, what a brilliant and crushing answer that would be to those who are constantly saying that social organizations can only be changed at the cost of violence and bloodshed! Gentlemen, I entreat you to examine sympathetically the memorandum which I shall bring before you I believe it to be the means of strengthening democracy and enlarging freedom not only in this country but throughout the world"

He sat down and took from his breast pocket typewritten sheets of paper which he distributed among his colleagues It was, for him, a proud moment, for these sheets of paper represented a plan on which he with others had worked for many years It was a plan by which the economic resources of the country were to be reorganized so as to ensure the maximum production that was consistent with a lowering of the hours of work The wealth produced was to be devoted solely to the needs of the producers, and full compensation was to be paid to all those who in the past had had the legal right to profit, whether willingly or unwillingly, from the disabilities of others It was the Professor's boast that his programme would leave no one the poorer, but would immeasurably increase both the material well-being and the spiritual unity of his fellow citizens There could be nothing wrong with the plan It had been approved in its every detail by appropriate experts. It was mathematically correct It had only to be understood.

"Please consider this plan at your leisure, gentlemen," the Professor said "And if you will meet me here to-morrow morning we will discuss it Meanwhile may I assume that we are agreed on my proposal for a plebiscite?"

The Chief of Police spoke for the first time since he had re-entered the room He smiled twice in quick succession and then said "I suppose you are aware, Professor, that your proposal will not be very kindly received across the frontier?"

"I do not mind how it is received there," the Professor replied "What is obvious, however, is that our enemies can have no kind of an excuse for intervening before the plebiscite; and after the plebiscite they will have, if possible, still less excuse for doing so"

"I can't help saying," said the Commodore, "that some of this programme of yours looks rather socialistic We don't want that kind of thing, you know"

The Trade Union representative had another objection to make "I see," he said, "that you have been stealing some of our ideas We shall have to demand due recognition for that."

"I beg you, gentlemen," said the Professor, "to confine your attention, if you will be so kind, to essentials We shall hardly need, I think, to discuss what adjective is most fitted to a description of my plan nor who were its original inspirers The point is, will it work better than our present organization? For my part I have no doubt whatever that it will But we shall discuss that to-morrow For the moment all I ask is your assent to my proposal for a plebiscite to be held at the earliest possible moment If I have your assent to this, I shall ask the Chief of Police to begin to make his arrangements at once There will be, of course, complete liberty for all parties to express their views in connection with the plebiscite, though not many people, I fancy, will dare openly to advocate the surrender of our country's independence"

"I should think not, the rotters!" pronounced the Commodore "Do you know, it's a most remarkable thing how things have changed since people gave up playing tennis Or it may have been the effect of the War Anyway there's not so much patriotism as there was I regard that as certain"

By now the other members of the Cabinet, having signified their assent to the Professor's proposal, had risen to their feet and were preparing to disperse The Professor himself could not help observing how undistinguished a group they formed He was glad now that he had not acted on his first impulse, which had been to demand the resignation of the Chief of Police, for Colonel Grimm appeared to be the only one of his colleagues who possessed the ability either to act or to think consistently. He was pleased, however, to notice that his plan for a plebiscite and his confidence in its result had infused at least some resolution and some degree of unanimity into the Cabinet Dr Tromp and the leader of the Trade Unions had left the room arm-in-arm and the Commodore, before following them, had brandished his walking stick as though it were a sword, pronouncing in a jocular voice the words "Up and at them!"

The Professor remained for more than an hour's conversation with the Chief of Police It would be possible, he found, for the plebiscite to be held after an interval of two days Until the plebiscite had been taken no mention was to be made of the Economic Plan, for a longer period for discussion would be needed, so the Professor thought, before that plan should be put to the vote Colonel Grimm appeared to have such a deep sympathy with his aims that at the conclusion of the interview the Professor made no effort to restrain the expression of his enthusiasm. For he seemed now to see his way clear to an achievement that would be new in the history of mankind— justice, established without bloodshed and by consent "And if, Colonel," he said, "our small country can make that contribution to civilization, to fight for its independence will be to fight for the future of the world" The Chief of Police smiled his two smiles "I agree with you, Professor," he said, "from the bottom of my heart"

CHAPTER IV

THESE PRETTY COUNTRY FOLK

THE Professor paused upon the stairs that led up to Clara's apartment It had suddenly occurred to him that of the crowds through which he had passed on his way from the Chancellory hardly one person in a thousand could possess any knowledge of classical literature Neither his friends noi his enemies, therefore, could have any clear idea of how the greater part of his life had been spent or what were the stimuli that provoked his most distinct and luxuriant emotions And he himself, what knowledge had he of the way of life of those whom he represented? He had inspected but never worked in factories, he had bought goods in shops but never sold them, he had enjoyed football, but seldom found time to watch the game, he was a teetotaler and a non-smoker "Justice," he whispered, stretching out his hands as though in confident appeal to some impartial court, "justice that can be demonstrated mathematically, that is what I have to give"

A gentle smile appeared to chase away the feelings of perplexity and apprehension that had momentarily invaded his mind He began to think of the woman whom he had come to visit, of the understanding and confidence which existed between himself and her, and he knew that if he was capable of makmg that rare contact with one other individual on earth, he was at least richer than many and perhaps also more wide awake to the distress of others,

He mounted the stairs quickly Clara did not rise from the place where she was sitting when he entered the room, but instead held out her hands to him smiling, as she tossed back with a movement of her head the mass of tawny hair that half shadowed her steady eyes, which, perhaps because of their intentness, had always seemed to the Professor more like the eyes of a man than of a women He took her two hands and kissed them

"Listen, my dear," she said, "I can see that you have something to tell me, but first of all will you help me with my Greek I know that this piece is quite easy and that it's beautiful, but I've lost my dictionary You know that I'm only a beginner"

The Professor looked at the book on her lap and at the passage to which she was pointing with her finger "It is beautiful indeed," he said "This is what it means" He leant over her chaii, and with his cheek close to her cheek began to translate, pressing his finger upon the paper by the side of her finger "No longer, maidens with throats of honey, voices of desire, are my limbs able to bear me Oh would that I were a kerulos who over the wave's flower flies, having a careless heart, the sea-purple spring bird"

"It is lovely," she said, and there was a silence between them Then with a smile she turned her head sideways to him and said, "Is it escapism?"

The Professor kissed her parted lips and then, straightening his back, stepped past her chair and stood facing her with his hands clasped behind him "When I was young," he said, "I used sometimes to get drunk On those occasions—there were not many of them—those words of Alcman would always come into my head They would intoxicate me more than the alcohol, not, I think, because of their rich sensualism, the honey and the desire, but perhaps more because of the swift flashing freedom of the last lines in juxtaposition to the weight of rather vague frustration with which the poem opens Escapism? I hardly think so No statement so direct can be escapist"

"You would like it for your epitaph, wouldn't you?" Clara said with a smile, but the Professor's face was serious when he replied, "If I dared, or if I were a poet"

There was a short pause, and then the Professor too began to smile "May I inform you," he said, "that you are speaking to the Chancellor?"

Clara's exclamation showed either pleasure or surprise She sprang to her feet and, as she stood upright, with her hands grasping the Professor's elbows and her head thrown back, her attitude for a moment might have been compared to that of a laughing Mænad, confidently passionate, barely in contact with some other being of whose existence she was only half aware and which might the next instant be destined either to be loved or to be torn to pieces The Professor himself was surprised at the strength of her hands' pressure on his arms, though almost immediately her body relaxed and, being taller than he was, she leant towards him and kissed him on the forehead, her chin just disturbing the upper rim of his spectacles "I am terribly glad," she said, and then, after she had sat down in her chair and motioned him to another she asked for the whole story

As the Professor told her of the Cabinet meeting, of the demands made by the Ambassador, and of his own plans for a plebiscite he found that her occasional questions and comments clarified for him as well as for her the whole situation. Never before had he come into contact with a mind that could so anticipate not only his own words but even the more indistinct thoughts and feelings that lay behind his words His conversation with her had a unique quality, a slender delicacy combined with a profound assurance, a quality which in his own mind he would compare sometimes with fencing, the intimate contact on a quarter of an inch of metal, sometimes with the delicious interpenetration of physical love She shared with him the apprehension which he was bound to feel when he thought of the weakness or stubbornness or stupidity of his colleagues in the Cabinet on whom, to some extent at least, he would have to rely for support She strengthened his own confidence in the result of the plebiscite and, a thing for which he was chiefly grateful, she appeared perfectly to understand the enthusiasm which he felt for the Economic Plan which he would put forward as soon as the plebiscite had made the country safe from the fear of foreign invasion He gave her a copy of his memorandum, and in voices that served to calm the excited agitation of their thoughts they discussed once more its prospects of success and the hopes that it might hold forth for the peaceful and orderly advancement of mankind

The discussion was interrupted while they ate sandwiches which Clara had prepared previously, and the Professor followed her lovingly with his eyes as she went about the room, as she poured out a glass of wine for herself, as she stopped over a gas-burner on which she was boiling milk in order to make him cocoa His eyes dwelt on the tense strong lines of her body, on the mane of hair that swung across her face, and the firm mouth compressed into something like seventy as her attention was concentrated on the saucepan And this moment may well have been the happiest in the Professor's life, for he believed then that he was in possession of the two things that he most desired, the power to benefit mankind and the freely given love of another being It was as though Clara had read his thoughts, for she asked suddenly: "Which would you rather have, me or the Economic Plan?"

The Professoi laughed "Which would you rather be, dead

or not alive? Fortunately, my dear, I don't have to choose between the two"

"No, but seriously," she said "Let us play the children's game and suppose that you had to choose"

"Well, then," said the Professor, "I could hardly ask you for your love if I had deliberately failed in my duty as a human being."

She crossed the room and sat on the arm of his chair "You are always right," she said as she gently slipped one of her long arms around his neck and meditatively, with one finger, smoothed the stiff bristles of his moustache

The increasing roar of a squadron of planes flying over the house aroused them to attend to what was outside the room "I have been hearing that noise all day," the Professor said He looked at his watch "What do you say to a drive to the >first bridge, and a short walk up the valley to the waterfall?"

Clara was pleased with his suggestion She hurriedly telephoned for her car and fetched her coat from the bedroom "Ought I to wear a hat," she asked him, "now that I am going out with the Chancellor?"

"Certainly not, my dear," said the Professor, "and, as a matter of fact, no one ever recognizes me outside the University"

They went downstairs to the car, and at the street door were saluted by a young police officer The Professor looked closely at the man, since he seemed to detect something familiar in his appearance But Clara was calling to him from the car and he followed her without stopping to think more of what might or might not have been a previous acquaintance They had soon passed out of the town and were looking with delight at chestnut trees, already sumptuous with their new green, loaded with the colour, at beeches whose brown buds were swollen to bursting and which were beginning now from their topmost branches to display, like flags, some few scattered and tender leaves, at the small yellow sprinkled like powder over the intricate twigs of birches and the more solid ginger of stiff-standing oaks In the fields they observed cows careering wildly, with extended tails, along the banks of streams, and beyond the fields, in the half-dressed woods, single cherry trees flung out their brilliant and delicately loaded arms One of these trees in particular attracted their attention and, stopping the car at the roadside, they decided to go no farther, but to

enter the woods, admire the blossom, and perhaps find some
secluded spot where they could he down, together in the sun

They crossed the soft, almost spongy, grass of the meadow and,
after the cries of the city and the subdued but continuous noise
of the car's engine, they seemed to hear the notes of songbirds
in an unearthly isolation ringing down to them through the
liquid air And in the woods beyond this sense of isolation
was felt more deeply. Sounds from the road, which was
scarcely half a mile away, were not so much interruptions of
their solitude as a barrier surrounding it For a second or
two, after they had passed the first black branches of the trees
and stepped upon a carpet of primroses and anemones, they
seemed to have been translated to a different mode of living,
an existence that was private, ghostly, and breathless, a state
between, on the one hand, the traffic-laden road. and, on the
other, the freshness and the melody that were fluid in the air
and among the tree-tops Neither of them spoke a word, but
Clara stretched out her hand and touched the Professor's thin
brown hand with her finger tips. The charm was broken, but
he was enchanted or bound in a new spell, his certainty of
understanding and his belief in love "There is nothing in the
Greek," he said, "which can describe this Our country is
more tender, perhaps more pure"

They had reached the cherry tree. Its black trunk was
crowned and over-bowed with a mass of snow, so that the
trunk appeared like a gash or ravine in some inaccessible peak,
although here what was difficult and not to be grasped was not
cold, icy surfaces, rigidity or lack of air but only the unexpectedness, the fragility, and instantaneous character of what was
seen. At a little distance from the tree was a bank of primroses
sheltered on three sides by bushes but now bright with the
afternoon sun Clara took the Professor's hand and together
they walked slowly to this bank and lay down side by side,
gazing lazily through sharp and crooked twigs at the whiteness
that seemed purer than air, and at the small clouds, less white,
that floated beyond across the blue After a while they turned
on their sides and stared into each other's eyes, cloudy, confident, and inebriated with delight "Ah, Helen," said the
Professor slowly, as with one finger he traced the line of her
nose, "from the regions which are holy land"

They were startled by the noise of crushed twigs and approaching voices The Professor sat up, but Clara remained indolently

lying as she was, and soon the Professor too relaxed his pose of attention and supported himself on his elbow. He had no desire to be an eavesdropper, particularly as he had recognized the voice of his son as one of the voices which were drawing near, but neither did he wish to emerge suddenly from the shelter of a bush with a lady, a course of action which might easily be considered compromising to them both

Through a gap in the branches the Professor saw the lean figure and flushed face of his son There was impatience and something like distress in his manner of walking and in the expression of his eyes as he turned his head to his companion, a young girl, dressed in green, whose pale face and yellow hair seemed equally luminous in the pouring light In her looks too, there was an intensity that appeared to the Professor out of keeping with the brilliant and enchanting mood of the day, The girl he recognized as one of his own pupils, a particularly promising one, who had won a scholarship to the university from a provincial high school

The Professor reflected that when he himself had been the age of these young people he would spend his afternoon walks in the eager and enthusiastic discussion of some such subject as the immortality of the soul or the disputed authenticity of a poem by Anacreon Neither of these subjects, nor anything like them, was, he could see, the topic of conversation between this boy and girl, who had passed across the gap in the bushes and had seated themselves beneath the cherry tree, out of sight but within hearing

Clara leant towards him, her hair brushing his face "All the lovers are out to-day," she whispered, and gently touched his cheek with her lips before she lay back again on the primroses with her tawny head, like a contented cat, restmg on one open palm, and her eyes closed

The voice of the girl beneath the cherry tree sounded both tired and aggrieved, as though she and her companion were reaching the end of a long and inconclusive argument "But I can't see," she was saying, "why we shouldn't enjoy ourselves"

"I would rather have a double whisky," said the Professor's son sharply, but at once his voice changed and seemed to express a feeling compounded of tenderness and exasperation "Can't you see," he said, "that I love you? I don't want you as an occasional stimulant I want you to be part of my life

And what sort of life have we now, I mean in these next few days, weeks, months, to look forward to?"

The girl spoke slowly "I understand what you mean," she said, "but I don't agree with you You are being chivalrous, or romantic, or perhaps are seeing yourself as an ascetic, the extreme sensualist."

"Damn your psychology," said the young man "Any or all of your words may describe something but they explain nothing I tell you for the thousandth time that to-day, now, in this country, love between two people is impossible, except as a drug, and so is peace"

The girl was on the point of tears There was no anger in her voice as she replied "I see that as well as you do Are we not in the same party? Don't we both work for the same things? Our life may be dangerous, but we share it together We are both devoted to politics and the revolution Isn't that a basis for enjoying love?"

"Devoted to politics," said the Professor's son. "Yes, as one might be devoted to death But we are devoted to them all right"

"I never thought I'd hear you say that," replied the girl, although it was perhaps the tone of voice in which he spoke rather than the words themselves which caused her to express both dissatisfaction and anger with him

The young man, too, spoke angrily "And do you really think that I enjoy the futile resolutions, the interminable discussions, the evasions, the intrigue, the hole-and-corner fighting in which we spend our time? Perhaps the flags attract you? Maybe you are impressed with literary critics Or does the word 'revolution' make you feel good?"

The girl had sprung to her feet Through the bushes the Professor could see her face and observed, with compassion, the tears in her eyes Almost above their heads burst out the brilliant short song of an early black-cap, but the two young people did not notice the bird They looked bitterly in each other's eyes for a moment then the young man stretched out his hand and began to speak in a voice that was rough with an interrupted tenderness "I'm sorry," he said" I'm speaking as though I were angry with you I am just as fond of flags as you are If I don't often love the work we do, I love the people with whom we are doing it, and I know that it must be done You are right in calling me romantic, because I think more of what I am able to imagine than of what I am forced to do. If the revolution had taken place already, if we had cleared away the cruelty and heraldic stupidity that now force our living into back alleys or into the mud, what could we do then, I keep on thinking, how would you look then, what work could we share, how disinterestedly could we love! But the love and work of construction and reconstruction are, for us, indefinitely postponed Our job is to destroy before we are destroyed ourselves And we must hate so that there may be a world for love And for us who follow the revolutionary idea neither love nor hatred can be always pure I used to think that our cause was just and necessary that all who were against it were desperately wicked, all who were for it were my true comrades Soon I observed that this was not so I had to see opposed to me, for example, my father, a man whose whole character I respect and who is divided from us only by the sharp edge of doctrine which he has the candour and intelligence to admit as a division, while on our side we have many who subscribe to our principles without understanding them, some psychological cases who enjoy intrigue and, even after the revolution, would no doubt continue their game But I did not at once see what this means It means that when it comes to shooting I shall shoot some criminals and some people whom I know to be better men than myself Why, then, should I shoot at all? Why extinguish any life which is, even in an enemy, wonderful? The answer is not quite so stupid as to be arithmetical. It is not simply a question of there being a greater percentage of good people on our side than on the other It is more the case that we are under the terrible and necessary dictatorship of an idea And this idea differs from many others in being wholly designed for application to the real world. It is the idea of humanity which, for a time, must submerge our own humanity We believe that our enemies, occasionally with the best intentions, are at the moment at war with us, even if they pretend peace; and we believe that our enemies must be destroyed or else they will destroy not only us but themselves and everything that makes life dignified and promising One is inclined to shrink back, is one not, from consciously repressing the human instinct to love everyone; yet that instinct must be repressed if one is to tighten one's finger on a trigger that will certainly release death; for it is most unlikely that one will find oneself face to face with any convincing incarnation of the evil which we desire to destroy More likely it will be some poor old aimless man or misguided boy whom we will deprive of life, or some wretched perverted Legionary, half-crazed and hysterical with myths of blood and bloodshed that are the only means he has of his disguising from himself his own panic War is a movement of masses in which the individual counts for less than his true value, and we are at war. That is why war is hateful, but we are still at war What does our purity or impurity matter? Isn't the revolution more important than our perfect integrity? Certainly Exactly I quite agree with you I am only saying that it would be nice if what was impossible could happen"

Some petals from the cherry tree drifted slowly downwards through the an. The birds were still singing, although the air was somewhat colder, and the Professor, peeping from his hiding place, could see that the girl had now sat down again close to his son's side and had linked her arm with his

"So we can never be happy?" she said slowly, though her voice this time expressed affection and more confidence than when she had last spoken It was as though she were resigning herself, almost with a sense of relief, to a defeat which had been represented to her in some dream as inevitable "I came to know you," she was saying, "as another person in the world like myself, and I could see that you were becoming aware of me in the same way You were the first person to whom I told my secret thoughts and in whose own secrets I shared as an equal, as a fellow creature approached deliberately with love. It is the way we grow up, I suppose, and perhaps neither of us would have grown up exactly as we did if we had never met But you are right I know you more intensely and with a greater delicacy than I know anything else; and yet it is not you who shape my life nor I who, when all is said and done, are more than an important incident in yours War is heavy, sultry, and oppressive, and it overrides us all. And when you say that just now, we being at war, you would rather have a drink than me I am not sure that you are not right, though a year ago you would never have said that Do you remember that time, on a day very like this, in a place not far from here, when you first made love to me? Though I had expected it, it was still sudden, and though I wanted words I was breathless I thought then of our ignorance and of our examinations, shrinking back just for a moment from the appalling novelty of love I was not afraid of you and it was not you that even partially I rejected; I feared and admired what was happening to myself Inexperience, I suppose, made that new happiness so sweet and piercing as to be more like pain Wonder made us stand back a time and admire the structure, as delicate as a living web, that bound us together I believed that structure was steel, but now I see that the steel is on the other side, fastening us to the war It is nothing so delicate as gossamer that ties us in the world of men and women, and we would have deluded ourselves if we had imagined that we were a world to ourselves. I wish we had deluded ourselves then Now it is too late We can no longer be worlds to each other. The love we Imagined demands peace It might have been fine and I wish that we had tried As it is each can afford the other pleasurable sensations, kindness, some tender memories; that is about all"

The Professor seized hold of Clara's hand, dragged her to her feet, and together with her almost charged through the bush So deeply was he moved that he hardly observed the look of astonishment on the faces of the two, young people when first they saw his head, hatless and the spectacles awry, thrusting through the leaves In his precipitation he tripped, before he was well clear of the bush, over ai root and fell prostrate at the young girl's feet She recovered from her surprise and was now smiling, as was Clara also, who had arrived upon the scene in a rather more dignified manner than her lover But the Professor had risen to his feet with the agility of a young man. There was a torn place in the knee of his trousers, but he did not notice it While he was still readjusting his spectacles he began to speak

"My dear children," he said, "please forgive an old man for bursting in upon your conversation Yet even I, as you see" (he turned and bowed to Clara), "am not too old for love How can you bear to reject it?"

He paused and observed in the girl's eyes a look of hopelessness and tears beginning to swell there His son's face wore that expression of bewilderment with which he was already familiar "Foigive me," said the Professor, "if I am trespassing on what is intimate I wished only to congratulate you" He smiled and the two young people also smiled, but without looking at each other, and in an awkward and embarrassed manner "And therefore take the present time," said the

Professor in his low, gentle, and musical voice. A kind of gaiety was expressed in the gestures of his hands as he continued "With a hey and a ho and a hey nonny no," and there was triumph, reverence and finality as he concluded "For love is crowned in the prime, in the spring time"

He stopped, for the girl had suddenly let her head fall upon his son's shoulder and was weeping bitterly, hopelessly, like a child The young man put his arm round her and stared above her golden head, hard-eyed and stiff-lipped, into the trees, and for a moment it seemed most surprisingly to the Professor that the sinking splendour of the sun, the scattered notes of birds the light breeze in the branches formed together with the pain of this boy and girl a whole scene or a consistent mood, and that it was he himself, with Clara, who was standing outside the picture The next moment the two appeared to him again as pitiful castaways, outsiders from the breathing warmth of the day "Come, Clara," he said, as he hastily took her arm, "we must be going We must not keep our chauffeur waiting"

CHAPTER V

MORALITY

IT was ten o'clock at night, and the Professor was walking back from the President's Palace to his own rooms in the College which he would leave on the following day in order to take up residence in the Chancellory A wind was blowing in great gusts, then dying away, as though it had been fired from a gun, for at one moment there would be a dead calm, though between the street lamps in the worst lighted districts one could see always the stars quickly traversed by high clouds, and then suddenly a puff of wind would explode at the end of an avenue and come running up the way, driving and scraping paper bags, empty cigarette cartons, leaves, and bumt-out matches into and along the gutters You could see men quickly lowering their heads and clapping their hands to hats, women turning their faces aside and wrapping their coats more tightly round their bodies The wind would whistle into side streets and cease. On the roofs of shops or of municipal buildings flags flapped angrily now in one direction, now in another, or were twisted and unwound around their poles.

The Professor had visited the President in order to receive

official confirmation of his appointment as Chancellor He had remained to have dinner with the old man who, as was soon evident, had little knowledge of or interest in the political situation The Professor smiled as he thought of the trembling fat creature, somewhat resembling a frog, who, twenty years ago, in a time of peace, had been given the office of President because of his knowledge of foreign languages and his reputation as a mathematician The President was now in his ninety-seventh year, his hearing was acute, but he was almost totally blind Moreover his memory was failing It was said that he had now completely forgotten the greater number of the fifteen languages, knowledge of which had secured him his elevation to the highest position in the state, and, since in the years immediately preceding this time the changes in the Government had been so frequent, it was perhaps not surprising that he was unable to distinguish between the last ten or twelve men who had held the position of Chancellor For some time he had imagined the Professor to be a certain general, long since dead and, though he had grasped his real identity for the duration of dinner, he had before the Professor left again relapsed into the same illusion

A gust of wind tore down the street and the Professor, as he turned his head sideways, saw beneath the lights, that seemed themselves to be swinging in the wind, a compact body of men marching down a side street towards him The bluster of the wind seemed to snatch into the air and scatter both the rattling of their drums and the few shouts of protest or anger with which people in the road or from their houses saluted the marching Legionaries

The Professor paused in the middle of the road to watch, but in a moment he felt a hand on his elbow and, turning his head, saw the same young policeman as he had observed that afternoon outside Clara's flat

"May I have a word with you, sir?" the young man said and, acting as though he were placing the Professor under arrest, he took him by the arm and almost forced him into the shelter of a near-by doorway Here they stood in silence, and the Professor again, as he looked inquiringly at the young policeman, was perplexed by something familiar in the man's face The heard the marching feet of the Legionaries reach the end of the side-street, then shouts of command and singing

voices going down the avenue in the direction away from the
doorway in which they were hidden

"What was it you wanted to say?" the Professor asked, and
began to step towards the road The policeman again laid a
restraining hand on his arm The Professor turned his head
and observed on the man's face a quick and almost boyish
smile that again reminded him of something which he had seen
recently.

"You would not make a very good detective, Professor,"
said the young man, "if you can't even recognize people who
have attempted to murder you"

The Professor looked more closely and saw that this was
indeed Sergeant Jinkerman without his beard or any of the
signs of age. Another gust of wind made him withdraw again
into the doorway and put his hand to his hat "If I may say
so, Sergeant," he replied, "I am getting a little tired of your
attentions May I ask whether the Chief of Police has found
some other job for you? Or what was your purpose in stopping
me in the street?"

Jinkerman's face took on an expression of severity which
the Professor realized would, with the mere addition of a beard,
turn to one of tragedy "I took you into this doorway," he
said, "in order to preserve your life And what worries me most
is that the Chief of Police has given me nothing to do"

"What on earth are you talking about?" said the Professor
He was beginning once more to doubt the mental balance of
the policeman

Jinkerman spoke slowly, with no trace of a smile "Do you
mean to tell me," he said, as though he were the Chancellor
and the Professor a subordinate, "that you don't realize that
you are in danger? I don't say that those Legionaries would
have murdered you if they had met you in an empty street,
I only say that they might have done so, and that it was shocking
foolhardiness on your part to stand staring at them like a sheep"
He noticed the Professor's look and added quickly "Forgive
my rudeness But there is no time to be diplomatic This is
my second point. Why is it that the Chief of Police has made
no provision for a police escort for you? I can only assume
that it is because he is not unwilling for you to be assassinated,
and therefore I have throughout the day been following you
myself Not that I have any particular love for you, or any
confidence in your government, but I know that your death

would be the signal for civil war and invasion And we are not strong enough to face invasion.

Here the Professor stepped into the street "I appreciate your motives," he said, "but I am afraid that I cannot listen to you any longer I don't believe that I have any enemies who would go so far as to commit murder, and I have absolutely no reason to question the patriotism of the Chief of Police. Consequently it would be most unbecoming for me to listen to criticisms of him from one of his own subordinates Some time I should be very glad to discuss with you your own political views, but at present I must ask you to leave me If I should ever require an escort, I will ask for your services"

Jinkerman's mouth smiled, but his eyes were big with astonishment as he looked at the Professor's face which expressed both kindness and severity, but chiefly a supreme self-confidence "If you should ever require," he repeated as though he were dreaming, and then stopped, saluted smartly, and walked away.

The Professor followed him with his eyes until he had gone some way down the street and, as he watched the slim figure receding, he heard once more above the whistle of the wind the hum of aeroplane engines Looking upwards he saw one or two red lights in the sky and determined that, on the next day, he would ask the Minister for War what was the purpose of these exercises He began to feel less irritated with Jinkerman now that the man had left him, for after all, he reflected, it was true that at the present time, with feelings running so high, any highly placed functionary might be said to be in danger In his own view, certainly, elaborate precautions would add to rather than diminish any danger that there might be, since the strength of the Government depended on its ability to appear self-confident and thus to inspire confidence in others But this view was no doubt rather too subtle to be appreciated by an ordinary policeman. Although it must be admitted that "ordinary policeman" was hardly a fitting description of Jinkerman who, if he was to be believed, was himself actively engaged in politics Extremists, thought the Professor (and his mind went back to his own son), are always apprehensive of some great disaster, and their words and actions, if repressed, wholly disregarded, or even treated unsympathetically, may easily lead to a state of affairs in which disaster becomes a possibility Yet law and order, steadfastly maintained and wisely administered, had such an overwhelming attraction for the mass of men that a Government would have to be, thought the Professor, either wholly bad or else curiously inept, ever to be overthrown by force

It was with these comfortable thoughts in his mind that he set out to walk the last hundred yards to the College gates He would take the earliest opportunity, he decided, to speak fully with Jinkerman, who seemed both honest and intelligent and who would, he felt sure, once he had understood the Economic Plan, entirely change his attitude to the present Government Jinkerman might even have some influence with the Professor's own son Surely those who were most alive to the present dangers would be the first to co-operate in the peaceful, scientific, and democratic measures which had been so painstakingly devised to meet those dangers and end them It was only necessary to explain, the Professor was thinking, when, as he was just turning into the short alley that led to the College gates, he collided with another pedestrian

"I beg your pardon, sir," said the Professor "I hope that you are not hurt," though considering the size and weight of the man to whom he was apologizing, it would have been most unlikely for him to have sustained any injury.

The Professor was confronted by a man with the stature of a giant, what would have been a very fine figure if the effects of height and breadth had not been somewhat marred by an excessive amount of fat and a drooping posture of the head "Why, Professor," said this man, as he stretched out his hand, "I was hoping I might meet you You haven't forgotten me, I hope"

The Professor took the extended hand He had to go back a long way in his memory, but now he had no difficulty in recognizing Julius Vander, the scholar and athlete who had, both at school and at the University, been sometimes a friend, sometimes an enemy, but always a rival Julius had been a celebrated footballer and oarsman, noisy, self-confident, a favourite with women; what was more remarkable was that, as a scholar, he had been almost, if not quite, as distinguished as the Professor himself Yet his career, after going down from the University, had been as obscure as the Professor's had been famous He had gone abroad and, though rumours of him had been heard from time to time—of marriages and divorces, or of appointments in the armies of foreign states—his life had apparently followed no consistent plan, and he had done nothing to justify the high hopes that had been held of him in his youth

"My dear fellow," said the Professor, "I am really glad to see you If you can spare the time, come up to my room for a few moments and tell me what you have been doing"

"Damn this wind!" said the other angrily, as a fresh gust nearly tore his hat from his head "Thank you," he added quickly, and repeated the words which he had used before "I was hoping that I might meet you"

He fell into step at the Professor's side, and as they went towards the gate the Professor noticed that his companion was walking with shambling, unsteady steps and that he smelt of whisky.

They passed through the gate and up the stairs to the Professor's room without speaking Here Julius Vander's eyes blinked in the strong light and glanced away from it to the rows of neatly bound books which covered the walls His thick lips smiled slowly and, as he concentrated his attention on the books, a flash of intelligence seemed suddenly to transform his pale and over-fleshy face "So you still read this stuff?" he said, without looking at the Professor.

"I hope you do, too," said the Professor brightly, but his guest appeared not to have heard the remark "Have you got any whisky?" he said, and then, while the Professor was fetching a decanter and a syphon from the cupboard, he added "I haven't read any Greek for years"

Without waiting for an invitation he helped himself to a large glass full of whisky and proceeded to pull an armchair into position before the fire The Professor was wondering whether this display of bad manners was occasioned by drunkenness, hostility, or perhaps a desire to appear unconstrained or even friendly; but this thoughts were interrupted by a feeling of surprise when he saw his visitor throw off his raincoat and reveal beneath it the black uniform of an officer in the National Legion

Vander had observed his look A slow smile spread over his face as he settled himself in the chair and placed his glass in a convenient position on the floor at this side Whether it was the effect of the drink or the warmth of the room, he seemed now to have lost his pallor His eyes were brighter and, when he thrust his head forward, the gesture made him appear energetic and alert. The Professor began to think he had been mistaken when, in the alley outside the College, he had imagined his companion to have been the worse for drink There was something ponderous about the jaw, something brutal in his thick lips, too much flesh on the cheeks, but eyes and forehead showed both resolution and intelligence

"You were thinking," he said, "that it was strange to find a man of my brains wearing this uniform"

The Professor sat facing him, in a recess at the corner of the fireplace He rested his elbows on the arms of his chair and pressed tightly together the finger tips of his extended hands A beam of light from the table lamp passed across his stomach, leaving his face in shadow "To be honest," he said, "I must admit that that was exactly what I was thinking"

Julius Vander stretched out his legs so that his boots projected over the fender He lay back in his chair "May I alter, or reinterpret your thought?" he said "You were thinking that it was strange that a man who was at one time good at examinations in Greek and Latin should be wearing this uniform."

"A man who was as good as you were," replied the Professor, "I should call 'intelligent' But don't let us haggle over words When I described you as 'intelligent' I meant (and perhaps I am speaking arrogantly) that you shared my own view of an belief in the ideals of European civilization which we have inherited from the Greeks almost in their entirety, although they have been modified by an admixture (I am afraid a very small one) of Christian idealism I am afraid that I meant that you were either a liberal or, at all events, not unsympathetic to the ideals of liberalism You might differ from me on methods, I imagined, but would hardly aim at an altogether different goal But perhaps I am misjudging your movement?"

"No," said Vander slowly, "you are not misjudging the movement You are merely speaking beside the point" He glanced again, with a certain contempt, at the uniformly bound volumes with which the bookcase was filled. "I ought not to have been surprised," he continued, "to find you still harping on those frayed and worn-out strings Peace, democracy, culture—all that clap-trap, I expect you believe in it."

He spoke so coolly, with such a judicial air, that for the moment the Professor was more surprised at the man himself than at the sentiments which he had expressed

"Surely," he said, "you must have become a very complete cynic if you can pretend to be absolutely indifferent to such things?"

Julius Vander laughed as he put down a hand to the floor for his drink "Come, come, Professor," he said, "you will be telling me next that you believe in God"

The Professor looked grave "It is true," he said, "that I belong to no religious organization, but I should hesitate before describing myself as an atheist And I should certainly subscribe, from the bottom of my heart, to the ethical ideals preached by the great religions."

Julius Vander interrupted As he spoke his words seemed to come to him more easily, he appeared now to enjoy speaking, as though he had found himself after a long time in front of an audience that was sympathetic "You call me a cynic," he said, "but I must remind you that cynicism is a mood for men who are disappointed in their hopes I am far from being that I merely say that I would rather have power, a good drink and plenty of women than international peace What is more I see every prospect of getting exactly what I want And meanwhile you go on mooning about 'ethical ideals.' I should have thought that of the two of us it was you who are the most likely to fall into the complete disappointment that is the right condition for a cynic You haven't even got the mediaeval faith in some almighty God who will, some time or other, step in and do something about these 'ethical ideals' which are supposed to have emanated from him. You will admit, I suppose that the 'ethical ideals,' when left to themselves, have been doing pretty badly these last few years"

"And what would you put in their place?" said the Professor gently. The argument, he felt, was pursuing a course that was perfectly familiar to him Indeed, he would have expected from Julius Vander some more original approach to the problem of morality

Julius seemed to have divined his thoughts, for he said at once "If you are expecting me to treat you as Socrates you are making a big mistake I can see no resemblance whatever, and besides I am not such a fool as those fellows were—what were their names? Callicles, was it, or Thrasymachus? (the Professor nodded twice)—anyway the chaps who gave one vigorous speech for the sane outlook of an acquisitive and unsatisfied man, and then allowed themselves to be trapped by the silly sophistries of Plato's ugly old Dutch Yes, I do share their view that all these 'ethical ideals' of yours are mere clap-trap, schemes, like marriage, to enslave the strong man in the interests of communities of second-rate pedlars, dreamers, twisters, and things that are still wanting to be back in mother's womb, but I'm not content simply to assert this view and then to argue on the assumptions of philosophical pedants who, out of cowardice, have rejected it When you asked me what I would put in the place of your ideals, you expected me, no doubt, to say I would put nothing in their place, that I would simply disregard them or, at the most, adapt them in some sort of a Machiavellian way to the furtherance of my own interests Well, you are wrong One is a little more scientific nowadays than they were at the time of Plato Certainly I have as much contempt as anyone could ever have had for the tricking weakness and hypocrisy of your ethical idealists, but I have enough sense to know that, contemptible as each one of them is individually, in the mass they are a force to be reckoned with They are part of my environment, like rocks and water. Will I put anything in the place of your ideals? Yes, I will I will put their direct opposites in their place And, what is more, people will like it"

There was a note of exasperation in the Professor's voice as he broke in on his visitor's speech, yet this exasperation, as he proceeded, soon gave way to the carefully modulated tones and the gentle utterances which he was used to employ in any discussion Indeed, as he observed Julius help himself to another drink during the course of his first few sentences, he began to feel that the views which he had heard expressed were the result of some secret grievance, exacerbated by an excess of alcohol, rather than a sincere statement of any coherent plan of life

"You are speaking hysterically," he began, "and if I may say so you are not even representing the theories of the party whose uniform you wear. That party, if I am not mistaken, claims (unjustifiably, in my view) to be the party that is to restore the old morality in its original purity, to fight for the family, the home, the nation They accuse me and extremists of the Left almost impartially of undermining the strict codes of behaviour which we inherited from what in my opinion was a less enlightened past You know that I am entirely opposed to the National Legion I believe that their programme, if it could ever be carried out, would destroy all culture and many of the ethical ideals of which you think so contemptuously But you must admit that the Legionaries themselves, on the evidence of their own propaganda, do not think as you do. Their morality, in its practical application, is certainly different from my own, but I have, what you do not seem to possess, one point in common with them—namely a belief in morality itself"

"Perhaps it has escaped your notice," said Julius Vander, "that their morality, 'in its practical application,' if I may borrow your words, consists in beating or otherwise torturing to death people whom they happen, for one reason or another, to dislike, in deliberately distorting or suppressing the truth; in burning books and pictures; and—what is very important— in doing all this with a profound sense of spiritual exaltation Personally I am not attracted by such 'practical applications' of morality. As I said before, all I require is food, drink, Women, and a certain sense that I am controlling my own destiny Perhaps I am a more easy-going person than most certainly I have no real enthusiasm for torture, and do not entirely loathe everything in the culture which you represent But in these respects I am, I flatter myself, exceptional, and this is the point which you are so apt to overlook Your philosophical apparatus is too rigid, your practical experience is too narrow for you to be able to grasp the exceedingly important fact that, although the man in the street pays lip service to your ethical ideals and even shows a hangdog respect for your classical scholarship, in his real being he hates, fears, despises, and detests both the one and the other. Please do not interrupt for a moment Allow me to explain, as briefly as I can, how this position has been reached I know quite well the arguments which you have ready for me at the tip of your tongue, and it will save us time if I dispose of them at once You will tell me, no doubt, that no society of men could ever have come into existence without the aid of that fellow feeling between man and man which makes possible an active co-operation in the tasks set to man by nature You will perhaps enlarge, and even rhapsodize, upon the growth of this simple community feeling into systems of ethical ideals, religions, poetry, drama, courts of justice, the whole paraphernalia which is described as 'culture' or as 'civilization' You will draw my attention to the fact that this culture, these ethical ideals, are not only

fine things to be contemplated by professional moralists or
aesthetes but have also a practical, even a technical, value
Without morality it would be impossible to construct a motor
car All very find and true, and what the hell has that got to
do with international peace, abstract justice, democracy, and
the rest of the Greek and Latin words?"

He paused to take another drink and the Professor observed
particularly his flushed face, his bright eyes, and a certain
eagerness in his expression He himself was feeling sleepy
He folded his hands and began to speak calmly, with his
customary politeness "Forgive me," he said, "if I have misunderstood you, but I should have thought that the answer
to your question was obvious You have admitted that
morality, in its rudest forms, is bound up with the very existence
of the community. Is it not true that just as the community
develops, so also must its morality? It is, apparently, the
abstract nature of my ideals to which you take exception Let
me remind you that if all ideals were realized there would be no
progress. I confidently hope, however, that many of my ideals
will be realized, at least to some extent Surely, Julius, you
will admit that we are no longer living in tribes Arising out
of the morality which you agree with, me is a natural product of
man's organization into society, there is a wider morality
which has been emphasized by the great religions. It is a
logical, but a most brilliant development of mere tribal feeling
to assert that love is the highest value we know, that all men
are brothers, whether in or outside the tribe. It is the 'ought'
constantly revivifying the 'is.' And at the present moment,
with modern technique, our unprecedented control over nature,
the moment has come, or so it seems to me, for such ideals as
universal brotherhood, international peace, justice, to be
carried for the first time in history into the realm of practice"

The Professor slapped the arm of his chair and looked, still
gently, as his visitor. It surprised him that Vander was staring
at him with an expression in which amusement and contempt
seemed equally blended. Vander said "I thought that befoie
long you would talk about religion, in which you do not really
believe, but which you use from time to time in order to bolster
up your own essential timorousness and hypocrisy. Perhaps
you'll tell me exactly what you're doing yourself about this
'wider morality?' 'Love is the highest value we know' Really
How many people do you love? 'All men are brothers' In-

deed. How is it then that you are living so much more com-
fortably than the other members of the great family? Those
books of yours, for instance, they'd fetch a good price Enough
to keep a nigger for several years, I daresay Oh, come off it,
Professor. Why not admit that you're living off other people
just as I am, and that you like it? But that isn't the point
"The fact that I'm a poor unworthy sinner,' you may easily have
the hypocrisy to say, 'doesn't show that morality is wrong'
All right I'm prepared to play the game by your rules and
avoid personalities When I said that I'd smash your morality
I meant it And when I said that I'd put its very opposite in
its place I meant it And when I said that people would like
it I meant that too. Shall I just explain those points?

"The root of morality, as we agreed, is the fellow-feeling in
a community How does that fellow-feeling arise? It arises
from the instinct of self-preservation and, later, from the
instinct to preserve everything that one has identified with
oneself—wives, children, property. Its chief emotional stimuli
are hatred and fear Its intellectual stimulus is always the
desire to secure some advantage

"As societies grow larger there arise within each society
groups and sometimes individuals with mutually conflicting
interests Naturally they fight, and the victors have at all
times imposed their own version of morality upon the van-
quished The law and order which they have imposed by force
of arms to meet their own interests are described as a universal
or natural law and order This is the origin of what you call
'the wider' and I call 'the artificial' morality Indeed, morality
must become artificial whenever it is made to extend more
widely than the real objective self-interest of an individual or a
group at war. A belief in God, for example, is a convenient
background for the domination in the real world of priests and
kings And please don't imagine that I have any pedantic
objection to the belief in God At certain stages of society,
monarchy was an efficient form of government. And if
monarchy is the best thing available for the majority, then
they're certainly entitled to their God into the bargain

"Nearly all men at all times—the strong strongly, and the
weak weakly—have acted in accordance with the real morality
whose springs are lust for life, fear, and hatred. The artificial
morality was designed, as it were, for internal consumption,
simply as a means for keeping people within a society in their

right places The real morality does not change, and is incapable of change. Its roots in man's being are too deep, for it springs from the ineradicable desires of the human body—blood, bone and senses It has the force of an instinct, the instinct to preserve and amplify one's own life It has more in common with hatred than with what you call love For it is, in its perfect form, the morality of the proud and lonely individual, who does not cringe when he is threatened with danger You call this the morality of the tribe, but it is really the morality of the Man For when has any tribe preserved its fellow-feelings for a moment longer than external pressure made unity a necessity for self-preservation? No, real morality is the pride of man in himself, in his possessions, and in the power he can exercise over others This is the deepest thing in man, has always been so and will always be so

"Artificial morality, on the other hand, is constantly changing, is always being improved upon by philosophical pedants and enthusiasts By this time it has become a purely intellectual affair, with no roots whatever in the real inner life of men and women I really don't know how the rot set in, but the process may have been something like this The real morality of the man merges, as we have said, in times of danger, and for the biologically important reason of self-preservation, into the morality of the tribe (fellow feeling for those on one's own side: hatred for the enemy) All very good Well, then, some mathematically minded old pedant must have come along and said to himself 'If it's a good thing to feel kind to a certain number of people, surely it would be a better thing to feel kind to more people' Like a mathematician he eliminated everything real, sensible, and vital from his calculations He took no account of the fact that 'feeling-kind-to-some-people' is a consequence of 'feeling-hostile-to-others' or, to use your terminology, that love is a consequence, or reflex, of hatred; and from that first mathematical, intellectual, sub-human point of view it is only a few steps to your own announcement that all men are brothers and that love is the highest value we know.

"Those statements would be neat enough if real life had anything to do with geometry. As it is, they are not only untrue, but cruel and dangerous The artificial moralists have taken no account whatever of the basic fact that men only unite, only feel anything at all like brothers, when they are

threatened from outside or when they have something specific
to gain from someone else by force War is a condition without
which real fellow-feeling could not exist. And you have the
face to propose peace as the goal of morality. Men are only
men when they add to their manhood by proving themselves
superior to others What fun would there be in having a woman
whom no one else wanted? And yet you say that all men are
brothers?"

There was a note of such hatred in Vander's voice as he said
these words that the Professor found that he had involuntarily
looked at the poker in the fender, his eyes rather than his mind
having been in search of some instrument of defence

Vander licked his lips and went on speaking "So much"
he said, "for what I might call the intellectual fallacy of your
argument. Now just consider what you and people like you
have done with it You have succeeded in imposing on the
man in the street your 'wider' or 'higher' morality, and the
man in the street, who is not a half-baked philosopher, loathes
it There are cases, no doubt, of people who have been so
hopelessly oppressed, physically or psychologically, that they
have swallowed your stuff like dope Some such an explanation
must be found for the temporary and partial successes, at some
periods of history, of Christianity If one has had all the
stuffing knocked out of one, there is, I suppose, a sort of con-
solation in pretending that one likes it like that. In general,
however, the ordinary man has had a natural and healthy
distaste for all this business of love and brotherhood, although
since most men have sheepish qualities, they have been content
to pay lip-service to the philosophers and sentimentalists In
fact only one thing has, in the past, saved people like you from
being hustled off the stage of history for good and all, and that
thing has been your characteristic timidity and hypocrisy.
You have never made any serious effort to carry your principles
logically into practice, and very lucky for you, too

"We now come to the situation to-day. As you say it is now
theoretically possible, owing to modern science, for all men to
live as brothers are supposed to live in your idealized and in-
tellectuahzed scheme of things Oh yes, I don't dispute that
for a moment With proper organization everyone could have
enough food and drink, there would be just the right amount
of highly educated women to go round, and all the world could
read Plato in the original Greek Everyone could work for

everyone else: there would be no more war. and the whole
world would be turned into one big jolly factory without an
owner, and with playgrounds attached. That is the kind of
ideal which at the present time has resulted from your faked
generalized morality You say you want to make men brothers
What you really want is to make them ants.

"Now who are the supporters of the practical application of
your 'wider' morality? Not in many cases the official prophets
It has become clear that this practical application would entail
the abandonment of privilege and of power. Consequently the
Bishops, who as a rule have always been men enough not to
take their religion seriously, are almost unanimously against
your proposals to force them to do what they say that they
believe. They, along with most 'educated' men, will denounce
your practical Christianity as Bolshevism or as atheism They
are quite right; for 'the wider morality' was never intended to
be applied. It is inconsistent with man's real character. And
besides, if your plans really did come off and if the world were
to settle down amicably to centuries of picnics, boating expedi-
tions, and cultural displays what would be the point of having
any Bishops? No, face the facts, Professor None of the
official experts on the 'wider morality' are on your side. All
you have are a few disgruntled and hair-brained intellectuals,
which, as I say, is to be expected, considering that the whole
basis of your creed is an intellectualist fallacy which has never
yet been adopted by any normal straightforward man.

"Perhaps you will say that you have the workers on your
side. Yes, you have some of them certainly, and they are the
people whom you choose to refer to, rather patromsingly, as
'extremists.' I must say that I have slightly more respect for
them than I have for you They, anyway, have the guts or the
intelligence to realize that they are in for a fight They have
definitely something to gain, namely the incomes and privileges
of people like you and me. And if the rest of us were to he
down quietly and let the Reds take from us what we have taken
from them, no doubt everything, from your point of view,
would be very agreeable. Need I tell you that we are going to
do nothing of the kind? And we happen to hold all the cards.
We not only have the arms, but we possess also another overwhelming advantage which I will, if you like, describe as
spiritual.

"Your Reds, although they have something to fight for, are

fighting for it on the spiritual basis of this false, artificial, and anti-human morality which you have taught them. They talk about peace when they are in the middle of a war. You won't find us doing that, for our great strength comes from the fact that we represent the morality which is older, more vital, and more specifically human than yours Our love is the emotion not of a dutiful intellectual but of a warrior in battle. It depends on hatred for the enemy. Our justice is nothing abstract: it is simply the joyful elimination from the face of the earth of those who oppose us Why is our propaganda so much more successful than yours? Partly because our aims are definite, sensible, and within reach instead of being vague, intellectualized, and extending into infinity; but more still because we appeal to the dark and vital and real forces in human nature which have so long been hypocritically oppressed by the teaching of men like you We show our followers how to regain their self-confidence as individuals by hating their enemies You offer them a whole world to love we give them a tangible minority to hate We do not pretend that all men are equal or that women are the same as men Consequently our audience is not one of castrated intellectuals Real men have known all along, in spite of 'the wider morality,' that power over others is the normal flowering of personality, and that women are conquered, not persuaded into lust by a common interest in Euclid. And what to my mind is really amusing is the fact that it is people like you who have prepared the ground for us.

"Your Christianity, your Platonism, your intellectualist culture have had officially a long innings. They are, as I have said, unnatural and unfitted to real men; but if their exponents, the wider moralists, had ever attempted in the past to apply their doctrines in practice, human nature might possibly by this time have been somewhat changed. Here we have to thank you for your hypocrisy For by continually repressing men's natural instincts for lust, hatred, and self-assertion in the name of a morality which you have never acted upon yourselves, you have fostered in the deep places of their souls such bitter hatred for you, your culture, and your religion that you would be trembling if you could understand a fraction of it.

"The trouble with you is that you are no psychologists, and that is why we shall smash you and your more dangerous allies, the Reds. For we appeal not to the intellect, or even to immediate self-interest, but to the dark, unsatisfied, and raging impulses of the real man. It is we who are, in a psychological sense, the liberators. The only freedom that you offer is economic freedom, a barren and dusty slogan which no one who is not an intellectual even understands

"So I say that where you preach abstract universal love we shall restore the polarity without which no emotion is more than the shadow of a thought We shall be united in our hatred for those who love indiscriminately Where you emphasize the unique value of each individual as a devoted servant in some sort of incomprehensible ant-hill, we shall give real individuals the right either to lead or to follow, and in both cases to keep their integrity and self-respect When, you in your sickly hypocrisy, talk of understanding and tolerance, we shall understand but not tolerate We shall give man the satisfaction to which he is entitled, the satisfaction of striking down his enemies like rats And since the basis of our action is unlike yours, psychologically sound, the masses of people will like it They are sick and tired of you and of your ways of thought, and in one moment all their enforced respect and complacency will turn to the vast relief of the practical enjoyment of hatred

"Make no mistake about it We shall be savage, bloody and unmerciful As I told you, I am exceptional in having a personal distaste for torture And when you see before your eyes sights which will horrify you—perhaps an elderly pianist of 'advanced' views being beaten to death with clubs, perhaps a public meeting for the burning of the works of Homer—then reflect to yourself that the forces which you see madly and brutally exulting in torture and destruction are the forces which you, you and the fest of the wider moralists, have nourished and brought up in men.

"Meanwhile those of us who are realists enough to know what men want (and it is nothing intellectual), who have the courage and ability to lead them to it, will stand back for a few days and allow the holocaust a necessary purgation with more in it of terror than of pity History will have seen the last of men like you And we, who believe in the real integral pride of the aspiring individual, will then take command Neither money bags nor intellectual and artistic pretensions will cut any ice With us. And there will soon be no more talk of international ant heaps or of the world becoming a big factory Those who talk enthusiastically about the masses will certainly remain among them as our subordinates either in peace or war. You will, if you are alive, lament the destruction of culture, of the idea of progress, you will call us barbarians Do you not see that men are crying out for barbarism, and that your culture decayed long ago? As for progress, we shall certainly put a stopper on progress towards the collective and amorphous ant-heap The progress which we have in mind is the progress of each live man for himself within his own life-time, progress towards greater wealth, lovelier women, more extensive power As for the remote future, we declare frankly that we are not interested in prophecy

"If you will examine my argument you will observe its dialectic character We propose to re-establish, on a higher plane, the morality of the ages of piracy For the leaders adventure, pride, and power; for the slaves what they most want, and what you have denied them, absolute certainty, the demand for complete obedience, and the hope of booty,"

Vander stopped speaking abruptly He lay back in his chair, as though exhausted by the effort of his long speech, and began, without looking at the Professor, to fumble in one of the pockets of his uniform The Professor, too, was silent He was attempting to estimate, as honestly as he could, the exact force of the argument which he had heard He had no thought of danger, and would soon, no doubt, have begun to question the validity of the Legionary's premisses and of the logical steps by which some of his conclusions had been reached But for the moment he was speechless, for something in him which was deeper than logic had been aroused or insulted by the words of Vander He seemed to glimpse the presence of forces whose existence he had always overlooked, just as, in a nightmare, the dreamer may suddenly become aware of some menacing object which frightens him more, perhaps, because its enormity has been so unaccountably unnoticed than because of its actual ability to inflict hurt

Julius Vander took a piece of paper from his pocket and handed it to the Professor "I must have your signature to this at once," he said "It is a declaration that you and your government have resigned" He observed the look of surprise and consternation on the Professor's face and smiled "As I told you," he said quickly, "I have some rather exceptional traits in my character One of these, I suppose, accounts for the fact that I am offering you your life I might, for instance, shoot you now We could still publish the account of your resignation in the morning, and no alteration in our plans would be required. As it is, I will undertake to get you safely out of the country in return for your signature Nothing you may do, I might add, will prevent us from seizing power to-morrow"

The Professor had risen to his feet with the piece of paper in his hand. Now it was indignation that made him speechless, indignation and a feeling of horror that the authority of the government and his own integrity could be so cynically affronted He spoke coldly "You should know me better than to imagine that I would, under any circumstances, accede to your demand"

He remembered that Vander had spoken of shooting, and glanced quickly towards the bell which was by Vander's chair. Even if he could reach it it would only summon belatedly some more or less decrepit College servant The Professor's eyes turned to the poker, but Vander too had risen from his chair and was standing in front of the fireplace. He now held a heavy revolver in his hand.

"If I could convince you," Vander began, "that our victory was certain—"

"That would make no difference," the Professor snapped He was filled with a sense of irritation which, curiously enough, reminded him of the feeling he had sometimes had when he had momentarily forgotten the precise meaning of some rare Greek word, a word, perhaps, signifying a bath-tub or a certain kind of fish Vander was looking at him oddly. He was about to shoot, and the Professor was staring in a puzzled fashion at his eyes. He noticed the swaying of the curtain that covered the door, and must by some change in his expression have indicated that he had seen something unusual, for Vander turned his head sharply He was too late, however. The Professor received vividly the impression of the straight-standing figure of Sergeant Jinkerman, taut and still for a moment within the room, then a sudden gesture, a report, and smoke Julius Vander doubled up and fell forward on the hearth-rug His great body was convulsed for some moments with a fit of coughing. Blood came from his mouth His eyes were contorted and his lips, over which he seemed to have lost control, were trying to enunciate words A spasm passed up the length of one leg and died away, as though the limb had been flicked into immobility by lightning His mouth, with protruding tongue, fell open and lay on the carpet like a huge sponge

There was no more movement

The Professor turned to Jinkerman, who was now standing at his side The young man's face was very pale and his lips tightly compressed With a sudden movement he put his two hands over his face, and the Professor noticed that his shoulders were heaving as though in grief He could think of no words to say, and so put his arm round the policeman's shoulders Soon the young man took his hands away from his face. "I had never killed anyone before," he said in a low and apologetic voice The Professor smiled and continued to pat him on the back Jinkerman took a quick pace backward. "Have you a lavatory here?" he said The Professor pointed out the door to him and then returned to the room to wait while Jinkerman was being sick He avoided with his eyes the big corpse of his old rival, but he could not help noticing the thickening stream of blood that by now had reached the leg of his writing desk.

CHAPTER VI

THE SILK DRESSING GOWN

THE Professor was sleeping uneasily For although in his waking life he had remained confident that no danger threatened so big that it could not be averted by his policy, yet at the back of his mind he must have known that, however true his calculations might be, the threat was there and the danger in suspense; and now perhaps, in his sleep, his apprehensions, freed at last from the barriers of will, returned to plague him with the production of dreadful images

It had been long past midnight before he could retire to his bedroom First there had been the corpse to remove Then he had attempted without success to get into communication by telephone with the Chief of Police. Finally he had left the whole matter in Jinkerman's hands, only insisting that, until it had been clearly proved that Julius Vander had been in real fact an officer in the National Legion, no steps beyond precautionary measures should be taken against that organization. With this resolution of the Professor's Jinkerman had been in violent disagreement, but he had preferred not to spend time in arguing, since the most important task of all was obviously to give the Chief of Police an account of what had happened, and in particular to make certain that on the next day the public services should be organized in such a way as to be able to resist what, if Vander's threats had had any substance, might be feared as an attempt at revolution Jinkerman was to return early in the morning He had left a detachment of police to guard the Professor's room, and this time the Professor had raised no objection to his plans So they talked of necessary procedure, with no word of the deeper feelings that had been aroused by Vander's words and by the killing at close quarters

Yet when Jinkerman had left it was the details of that scene in the small room, and no thoughts of the general situation, that kept crowdmg upon the Professor's mind His memory presented most emphatically to him the great difference between the movements of Vander's lips in normal life and in the agony of instant death He saw over and over again the quick gesture of the arms which had brought Jinkerman's hands from the sides of his body to cover his face And when he had got into bed and extinguished the light, he felt an unreasonable impulse to switch it on again in order to make certain that the stream of blood had not, as he knew it had not, filtered over the carpet and under the door that separated his bedroom from his study

He began, in an effort to calm his mind, to recite to himself the first two or three stanzas of Keats' *Ode to a Nightingale*, but, though he seemed to see with great vividness the words printed on shining paper before his eyes, he either missed their sense altogether, or found that when a phrase was understood it gave him no pleasure. For some reason or other he whispered to himself the words "Beauty" and "Truth," but when he had pronounced the words they seemed to bear no reference to the scene which had been just enacted

He threw off the eiderdown from his bed and turned with closed eyes to the wall In what was half a dream he seemed to see a huge monument on a hill, and beyond the hill the sea in the distance, slopes covered with heather, and light fleecy clouds passing over a wind-washed sky. For a moment he sought vainly in his memory for the name of the person in whose honour the monument had been erected, and then he observed that a file of men and women, as numerous and, in the distance, as tiny as ants, was approaching the monument over hills and valleys for as far as he could see All these men and women were encumbered in one way or another. Some were dragging children by the hands or carrying them in awkward positions beneath their arms; others were bowed down beneath the weight of gladstone bags, iron fire-guards, clothes-horses, chairs, tables, piles of newspapers, or broken bicycles; and yet there was nothing amusing in the sight of so oddly equipped a procession, for in everyone's eyes was a dull look of fixed determination, and the straggling army was so vast that it would have been folly to have supposed that it was not marching to some useful end

As the procession approached the monument the Professor could not help observing some symptoms of perplexity and irresolution among the vanguard The monument itself shone with peculiar splendour, and the Professor remarked, without reading, the gold lettering which adorned its base He looked again at the crowd, and saw that each man, woman, and child, on approaching the summit of the hill, had thrust the right hand under the cover of shirt, cloak, or blouse The Professor was overwhelmed with a feeling of pity for this huge gathering, with their rugged, perplexed, harassed, or indifferent faces, but this feeling gave way almost at once to one of horror He had realized that they would all when the monument was reached tear out from their breasts their hearts, and move on again across the country, a much more ghastly procession than before And this certain knowledge of what was to happen, horrible as it was, was less horrible to him than the uncertainty as to what in particular each person would do with his or her heart once it had been wrenched from the flesh They might lay the red muscle reverently at the basis of the monument or hurl it, still pulsating, against the stony ground The Professor could not bear to wait and see He opened his eyes quickly and fixed them on the dull gleam of a piece of metal in his window that had caught the light of a distant street lamp

After some moments he closed his eyes again and soon slept, though an observer would have seen him toss restlessly from side to side of his narrow bed, for his body was over-tired and his mind, exhausted by the events of the day, was labouring still more under the weight of the menace of the day to come He seemed to hear in his ears a roaring, like the noise of aeroplane engines that he had remarked on several occasions during the last twelve or fifteen hours The silence, when this noise died away, was most agreeable, and it was in a refreshing calm that the Professor seemed to see a white panther moving at a beautifully graceful trot along a forest path The scene was so vivid that he remembered noticing bees and dragon-flies that hovered soundlessly over the bell-like shapes of tropical flowers, and he himself seemed to be moving silently and invisibly as he accompanied the slender and powerful creature along the long track through the woods He noticed now with a mild dismay that parties of Indians were keeping pace with the panther, sheltering themselves behind bushes on each side of the path, and running rapidly, with the quick excited movements of insects, from bush to bush in order to keep up with the animal who still trotted quickly and directly forward, seeming quite indifferent to its pursuers

The Indians were armed with bows and arrows, and from time to time one would kneel down and shoot at the panther before running to rejoin his fellows in the shelter of the next bush. The Piofessor observed distinctly that as each arrow struck the gleaming white coat a fleck of blood appeared, and yet the panther never turned its head, nor altered its gait There was a beautiful rhythm in its movement as it went on farther and farther, still accompanied by its jerky but untiring antagonists. The Professor thought to himself that the distance already traversed must be immense, and a feeling of pity for the wounded animal, whose delicate white was now deeply marked with red, flooded into his mind. Perhaps it was the unreality of the whole scene that brought it about that this pity, which he felt so acutely, caused him no pain but had on him a refreshing, soothing, and almost luxurious effect; and yet, though he was invisible, he could feel tears in his eyes as he watched the chase continue and the quarry so deeply wounded and so unmindful of its wounds.

But as the whiteness of the panther seemed to be changing entirely into red the Professor found himself transferred, with a suddenness that was in no way startling, to another scene in which white was the predominating colour and in which he was himself playing an active part. He was in a court-room—and standing on his feet He wore the gown and wig of a barrister and was in the middle of a speech of which the purport was so urgent that the actual words he was using made no impression at all upon his mind The room was wide and airy, and as he turned his eyes around he thought to himself that the panther, whose pursuit he had just witnessed, might be expected to be present at or at least connected in some way with the proceedings of the court. The walls of the room were white and shining; the desks close to him had been kept scrupulously tidy, although there was no one standing or sitting at them The court, in fact, might have appeared empty; but the Professor was addressing his speech to a large white tent-like structure, somehow reminding him of the decoration of an altar, which appeared dimly at the upper end of the room Behind this cloth he knew were the judge and jury; nor was he the least embarrassed by the fact that his audience was invisible. He was speaking with the utmost earnestness in favour of Julius Vander, though he was by no means clear as to the nature of the crime with which Vander had been charged, nor, as has been said, of the precise words which he had been using in his defence Suddenly he observed a movement in the draperies of the structure that had reminded him of a tent, a throne, or an altar Curtains he knew were being pulled aside, and in a moment the figures of judge and jury would be revealed His mind was overwhelmed by the realization that all this time he had been speaking in Greek, a language which, without any question, would be unfamiliar to the whole jury And the next instant he had become aware that the judge himself was in this case no public official, but actually Julius Vander himself The Professor now began to remember the words which he had been employing in his speech Much of what he had said might, he saw, be construed as an attack on the theory and the administration of justice. His position was quite hopeless; but more terrible than the thought of this was his uncertainty as to what he would see when the curtains were drawn back and the seat of justice exposed He did not know whether Vander would appear alive or as dead He strained his eyes to see as the curtains parted in the middle and were drawn upwards at the side, but now the whole court-room began to grow dark and he could only distinguish the dim shapes of arms, legs, and beards It had become impossible to recognize at that distance any single face or feature when the Professor observed that there was now standing at his side the naked figure of Miss de Lune, who put into his hand a sheet of paper covered with typescript In the fading light he attempted to read what he took to be either a resolution submitted for his approval or else a copy of some important instructions. His eyes encountered the words "While you are attempting to escape" and he turned at once to remonstrate with Miss de Lune, though on what precise grounds he would have found it hard to say

But now the whole scene had changed. He was standing at
the border of the sea surrounded by women who were hopping
and bouncing eagerly to and fro The nature of their movements surprised him until he realized that they were not women
but birds It was with a sense of immense relief that he envisaged
the arrival at any moment now of the poet Alcman, and yet
there was an element of uncertainty in his feelings, for the
scene was by no means one that he might have expected. The
dancing women, or birds, moved in a thick grey mist, and over
the surface of the sand were scurrying, just out of sight, the
spider-like shapes of crabs with eyes protruding on long stalks
from their heads. Every now and again the Professor would
recognize for a moment Clara in one of the dancers, but when
he attempted to approach her she would vanish with a quick
hopping motion among the throng, or else he would discover
that the figure which he had mistaken for hers was really that
of a stranger His feeling of uncertainty was growing greater
when a cry went round among the dancers "The Peacock
The Peacock!" There appeared disconcertingly the incongru-
ous figure of the Commodore, riding on a large bird with
drooping tail, and brandishing above his head an umbrella
A single bird-like note, neither harsh nor particularly melodious,
rose from the women With one accord they rose, without
wings, into the air and passed by the Professor looking, as they
went, into his face There was now no doubt of their inhumanity, for their faces were the faces of owls, and as they
passed him in quicker and quicker succession his feeling of
perplexity gave way to an increasing sense of horror. He tried
to put his hand in front of his eyes to avoid the sight of the
crooked beaks and thick feathers, but he could not move his
hand until the last of the creatures had flown past, and then he
found himself suddenly wide awake, with the sunlight streaming
on his bed through a chink in the curtain

Though he had not rested well, he was glad to be awake, for
he could now smile at the improbable terrors of his dreams, and
in particular could satisfactorily explain to himself the strange
intrusion of the Commodore into the world of his sleeping
mind; for he could hear distinctly from the next room the
booming note of that gentlemen's voice

"But it is imperative that we see him at once," the Commodore
was saying, and then came the muffled voice of the College
servant who at this hour was, no doubt, laying the Professor's

breakfast and was now insisting that until he had finished his work the Professor should not be disturbed

There was another voice, confident and rather contemptuous. "My good fellow, do you know who we are?" This was the representative of the Orthodox Trade Unions

The Professor got out of bed "I shall be with you in a moment, gentlemen," he shouted through the door He washed quickly, carefully brushed his thin hair, and then somewhat shamefacedly attired himself in a crimson silk dressing gown It was a garment in which he felt, even in the presence of the College servant, ill at ease Its flamboyancy, he could not help thinking, was more suited to the character of some arrogant and amorous grandee than to a man of his sober and unpresuming disposition But the dressing gown had been a present from Clara who had playfully insisted, when she made the present, on carrying away with her the old grey garment in which the Professor had eaten his breakfast for nearly twenty years, and which he secretly preferred to the resplendent gown which, so Clara said, made him look like a Cardinal Indeed she would, when she saw him in it, address him as "Your Eminence," a witticism which was not entirely pleasing to him, since he had all through his life been opposed to the institution of hierarchy The Professor smiled now as he thought of Clara, and with the tips of his fingers lightly stroked the glass that covered the photograph of her which he kept on his dressing-table He then went quickly to the door and entered the sitting-room

His movement was arrested by a momentary shock when he saw the large figure of the Trade Union leader standing in front of the fireplace in the same spot as that in which he had last seen Vander The Professor quickly recovered control over his memory, he glanced at the table where his breakfast was already set out, and then at the Commodore who was standing at the other side of the table, leaning on his stick He was evidently agitated by some strong emotion, for he beat the floor with his stick and was beginning "Look here, sir," when he broke off and said "Good God, Professor, you look positively like a film actress"

The Trade Union leader also seemed for the moment to have forgotten the purpose of his visit He approached the Professor and between his finger and thumb took hold of the skirt of the dressing gown, then dropped it as though the crimson had really been on fire "Imported," he said, and

went back to the fireplace where he stood, with his arms behind
his back, gently swaying on the soles of his feet, and effectively
shutting off the fire from the rest of the room

The Professor sat down at the table and began to pour
himself out some coffee "I imagine," he said, "that you must
have some urgent business with me Please forgive me if I have
kept you waiting"

The Commodore had now recovered from the shock of
seeing the Professor attired in crimson "Look here, sir," he
said, "what is the meaning of this?" and he put down on the
Professor's plate a leaflet of which the head-lines, printed in
large type, read: "Professor plans civil war," "Breakdown of
Government authority," "Save your savings"

"This puts me in a very awkward position," said the Trade
Union leader in a perplexed voice, but after these words, the
tone of which was almost plaintive, he drew himself stiffly up
to his full height, turned slightly sideways, and began to speak
as though he were addressing an imaginary audience. "Sometimes," he said, "I am accused of being on the Left Sometimes
I am accused of being on the Right. In reality I occupy a
central position"

The Professor was not listening to him A glance through
the pamphlet which he was holding had made it clear to him
that someone or other must have betrayed to his opponents
the memorandum which he had submitted yesterday to the
Cabinet Ministers. The pamphlet contained a complete list of
the economic measures which he did, in fact, intend to recommend to the people, but these measures were presented in such
a way as to make them seem, both in intention and in effect,
most unlike what the Professor and his advisers knew them to
be Where, for example, the Professor had recommended that
private interests in the State Bank should be bought up in the
name of the state, the author of the pamphlet asserted that the
Government proposed to take over the Bank after they had
confiscated the people's savings. Every one of the Professor's
own proposals had been expressed in the form of, first, a statement of the desired end and, secondly, a careful exposition of
how this end could be obtained without injuring the economic
interests of anyone. All these explanations were omitted in
the pamphlet, with the result that a reader would receive the
impression that the Professor had actually aimed at destroying
those interested people whom he had been, in fact, so scrupu-

lously careful, when he had composed his plan, to leave without any just sense of grievance. Finally it was suggested that the proposed plebiscite had been planned, not as a demonstration against the foreign enemy, but solely as a means to vest the Government with dictatorial powers And as a matter of fact, concluded the author of the pamphlet, any intervention against such a Government as that of the Professor and his advisers, even supposing such intervention to come from across the frontier, would be welcomed whole-heartedly by the masses of the people

The Professor started with surprise when he reached the end, for the pamphlet was printed above the signatures of the representative of the Orthodox Trade Unions and of several of his colleagues In his agitation he swept his hand across the table and upset the jug containing hot milk over the trousers of the Commodore, who emitted a short howl and then hopped on one leg across the room, holding tightly between finger and thumb, and pulling away from the flesh of his thigh, the affected portion of his trouser-leg He sat down on the edge of an armchair and attempted with a pocket-handkerchief to remove the stains Meanwhile the Professor had turned to the Trade Union representative "I should never have believed, sir," he said, "that you could have been guilty of an act like this"

The Trade Union leader swung round and gave the Professor a look in which a kind of bovinity was mingled with accusation "If you accuse me," he said, "of having had part or lot in the production of a document of this character, you are ranging yourself amongst my bitterest enemies"

The Professor saw that the man, in his peculiarly ponderous way, was telling the truth "You mean," he said, "that you know nothing about this?"

"Neither I," said the Trade Union Leader, "nor any of my colleagues. We are opposed to a dictatorship either from the Right or from the Left As the poet says, 'an enemy hath done this'."

The Professor turned to the Commodoie "Perhaps you, sir, can throw some light on this matter," he began, but the Commodore was still scrubbing vigorously at his trouser-leg "I say," he said, "have you got any benzine?"

The Professor had no longer any appetite for breakfast He rose from his chair and began to walk slowly, his hands clasped behind his back, up and down the room. He was speaking as much to himself as to his colleagues

"The circulation of this pamphlet," he said, "must be stopped at once This is not a question of curtailing the liberty of speech or expression It is a case of pure and deliberate mis-representation and, as such, it cannot be tolerated How many copies of this thing have been distributed already? Have either of you any knowledge of its authorship?"

He stood still in front of the Commodore, who had now adjusted his dress to his satisfaction and was sitting forward on his chair, his chin pressed to the handle of his walking stick which he gripped between his knees, while with the fingers of one hand he smoothed the ends of his moustache He seemed to discover rather from the Professor's attitude than from his words that he was being addressed "It's a funny thing," he began, "but I was saying only yesterday to my secretary—or was it my secretary? Upon my word, I believe it was to my wife. Or was it? Anyway, let that go. I was saying that I shouldn't be at all surprised if something like this were to happen What I mean to say is, Professor, that you're very good at thinking out schemes—brain-work, I mean, and all that, if you understand what I mean, but that's only half the battle you know, in fact a different kettle of fish altogether It all boils down to this, if you catch my drift You can think out a damned clever scheme Take this Economic Plan of yours, for example But who's going to understand it? Why, I can't understand it myself As a matter of fact I thought it looked pretty sticky when I glanced through it last night, I mean almost socialistic; but, of course, we all know that you're not a Red, so I didn't really bother to read it Now stop a minute Here's the snag Other people aren't so broad-minded Here, for example, comes along another chap, pro-bably quite a clever fellow, and twists the whole thing round in this pamphlet so that people will think that you've sold yourself and us to the rag tag and bob-tail A damned bad show, naturally, but the point is that this was just what I'd expected all along You can't be too careful with these plans that no one can understand You're brainy enough to understand it yourself, of course, but the point is that another brainy chap can easily come along and make the whole thing look foolish So where are we?"

He paused as though he had made a final analysis of the

situation and, before the Professor could reply, the Trade Union leader had crossed the room and began to shout angrily into the Commodore's ear, "If I understand you aright, sir, you are endeavouring to impugn the people's ability to discriminate between divergent policies"

"I don't know what the hell the fellow's talking about," said the Commodore, looking up at the Professor and affecting to ignore the presence of his colleague "And, anyway, he needn't shout"

"I would not shout, sir," roared the Trade Union leader, "if it were not for the fact that you are always pretending to be deaf"

The Commodore sprang up from his chair with unusual agility His moustache seemed to flutter as he set his jaw and fixed the Trade Union leader for a moment with a quelling eye Then "You may boil your face, sir," he said sharply. "Yes, sir," he continued, while the other man stared at him in speechless astonishment "You may boil it as soon as you like, and when you have boiled it you may cut it into little pieces You may sprinkle salt and pepper on it, sir Make it into a salad, in fact Jolly good idea Damn you, sir!"

"Gentlemen, gentlemen," said the Professor, "this is most unseemly Surely we have rather more important things to consider than our own feelings"

He had stepped between the two antagonists in order to avert what he feared might become a fight and, being a small man, was by no means confident that he would be able to restrain the huge Trade Union leader should he desire to use physical violence against the Commodore But to the Professor's relief the Trade Union leader had, after his initial shock, withdrawn into a pose of outraged gentility. He now spoke in low, almost painfully offended, tones

"Low personal abuse," he said, "is, I find, a characteristic of the so-called upper classes Personally I have always set my face against it, occupying, as I do, a central position I have never been so insulted in my life But I am not angry with this man No, I pity him"

"You can boil your face, sir," interjected the Commodore doggedly, as though he were in possession of some unanswerable formula

The Trade Union leader turned to the Professor. "That last remark, sir," he said, "shows such extraordinary ill breeding, such bad manners, that I am afraid I can no longer associate with such a person For you, personally, Professor, I have great respect, but I must beg you to accept my resignation at once"

"Damned good riddance," shouted the Commodore, "of damned bad rubbish!"

"For heaven's sake, gentlemen!" said the Professor. Even his patience was now almost at an end "Can we not avoid this childish behaviour?"

The Trade Union leader gave him a look of gentle reprobation. His voice was becoming milder and milder. "I am very sorry, Professor," he said, "that you should think that there is anything childish in the forbearance that I am showing What you have said strengthens my resolution to leave the Government"

He began to move towards the door The Professor hurried after him. "Don't go," he said "Of course, I agree that you were provoked in a most inexcusable way."

"And yet," said the Trade Union leader in the gentlest of voices, "you call me 'childish' I am very sorry Very sorry indeed I am going"

"You're a sissy," said the Commodore, for he had observed that his enemy had begun to speak in a voice that was becoming almost tearful.

The Professor, his attention divided between the retiring Trade Unionist and the angry old man who was now brandishing his stick as he stood before the fire, said in an authoritative voice, "Don't be a fool, sir!"

"Oh!" the Commodore shouted, and the Professor's attention was diverted to him, even though the other cabinet minister was by now disappearing out of sight "Oh! I'm a fool, am I Well, you can boil your face, too, sir. Yes, sir, and send it to me by parcel post" He began to stump towards the door "All right," he said, with his hand on the door handle, "you needn't worry I'll resign, too. I never wanted to be in the Government anyway and, if you ask me, it's getting a bit too risky nowadays And I don't think much of your Plan either, sir I shouldn't wonder if that fellow who wrote the pamphlet isn't quite right Good-bye, sir! Damn you, sir!"

He went out, slamming the door behind him, and the Professor could hear the footsteps of both Ministers clattering down the wooden staircase. He opened the door and was confronted by the two policemen who had been stationed there by Jinkerman as a guard. They saluted, but their action was

marked by the slightest hesitation, for the sudden appearance
of the Professor in crimson silk had evidently not corresponded
with the preconceived idea of him which they had had in their
minds For a moment he thought of following his two colleagues, but he reflected that they were both just now too
incensed to be able to listen to reason, moreover his own
appearance in the streets, dressed as he was, could conduce to
no good result.

He went into his bedroom and with a sense of relief deposited
the silk dressing gown on his bed While he put on his clothes
his mind was moving rapidly, for he was already becoming
aware that as things now stood every second of his time was
precious and every moment dangerous

CHAPTER VII

FATHER AND SON

WHEN he had finished dressing he went back to the sitting-room
One of the windows opened on to the College quadrangle, and
as the Professor passed this window he saw his son walking
quickly across the empty space towards the door of his lodging
The young man's head was bent forward so that the face was
invisible to his father, but there was something, not only in the
distracted movements of the arms and tension of the whole
body, that made him appear like a person bringing urgent and
almost certainly bad news For a moment the Professor was
reminded of the acting of certain undergraduates who had, at
one time or another, taken the parts of messengers in his productions of Greek plays—of one whose spasmodic movements
had excellently reflected the mood of the distraught Medea, of
another whose tense bearing had well suggested the horror that
a spectator must feel when contemplating the gradual entry of
Pentheus into a path leading inevitably to the most appalling
disaster. Yet this was his own son, he reflected, and, imagining
him to be in some trouble, he began to feel at the same time
sorry for the boy and nervously apprehensive as to how he
himself would be able to express his feelings should his son
ask for advice.

The Professor was a man naturally most tender of intimacies,
most chary of intruding in any way on the deeper workings of
a mind which he did not wholly understand Indeed, in respect
of personal relationships, it was not enough, he felt, to under-

stand or to sympathize only when deep feelings were actually
shared could one be justified in obtruding oneself upon the
secret place of another mind.

He looked at the telephone on his table, for he had been
about to ring up the Chief of Police in order to tell him about
the defections from the Cabinet and to inquire what steps had
been taken to prevent the further distribution of the pamphlets
Now he would have to wait. He heard his son's steps on the
stairs and, going to the door, instructed the guards to allow his
visitor to enter.

The expression on the young man's face was not like anything
which the Professor might have expected The mouth and chin
seemed to denote sullenness, almost an unwillingness to betray
a secret, and yet there was something in the eyes that suggested an overwhelming eagerness and urgency to speak.
Various explanations might have been found for such a conflict
in the mind, but what impressed the Professor most was a
look in his son's face which suggested horror, as though he had
recently walked into a ghost or only just awakened from a
nightmare No ordinary affair of College discipline or even of
disappointed love could account for so much distress and
confusion It was important, the Professor felt, to attempt to
set the young man at his ease

"There is something I want to say to you," the young man
began in a voice that, in his effort to control it, was stilted and
almost hostile.

The Professor smiled and pointed to a chair. "Not a redefi-
nition of the Polls?" he said gently, and at once realized that
he had made a mistake in attempting to be, even if ever so
slightly, funny

The young man had apparently taken his remark seriously
"No," he said gravely. "That is not the point"

The Professor, too, adopted an expression of gravity He
waited, and again was surprised at the evident conflict of
emotions expressed in the boy's face What remote and un-
realized inhibitions, he wondered, were restraining the words
that seemed to be boiling to his son's lips? But it was in a very
calm voice that his son proceeded "You remember the girl
whom you saw with me in the wood yesterday?"

The Professor felt, for some reason or other, relieved. "Yes,
certainly," he said. "And I should like to say that I have the

greatest possible respect for her A very acute and sensitive brain, if I am not mistaken"

His son continued as though he had not heard his father's words "I don't know," he said, "whether you are aware that she, as well as I, belonged to the revolutionary organization"

"I'm not surprised," said the Professor, smiling "Great minds, you know" Once more he became aware that he had been intolerably tactless How could he, he wondered, when speaking to his own son, be betrayed into mistakes of expression that he would never make if he were conversing with a stranger? Fortunately, he reflected, his son was too much distraught himself to take much notice of the absurd and unpardonable witticism

The young man now appeared to have crossed, as it were, some Rubicon in his mind and was speaking more fluently "She was doing some political work last night," he said "I was doing the same thing myself As a matter of fact we were distributing a pamphlet urging the workers to be on their guard against a possible *coup d'etat* from the National Legion We were attempting to rally everyone we could behind your Government That's by the way. I was working in the next street to her and didn't hear what happened till afterwards She ran into a troop of National Legionaries and they took her to tneir barracks Well, you can imagine what happened"

The Professor, who was sitting at the table, made the interrupted gesture of stretching his hand out towards his son His face expressed horror, pity, indignation He spoke very softly "My poor boy, and must I imagine the worst?'

From the tone of his son's voice it might have appeared that it was he who was now disinterested He spoke calmly, as though he were relating an ordinary narrative of events which had taken place somewhere else or at a different time "Yes", he said, "you must imagine the worst if you imagine rape and torture as the worst things" Only by the hurry with which he went on to the next sentence did he betray his agitation "They let her out late in the night," he continued "I did what I could for her, got hold of a doctor and all the rest of it She was too dazed to take much in But that's not the point"

When he paused the Professor began speaking, as much to himself as to his son "But this is monstrous," he said "This is terrible I could never have believed it Poor girl! My poor boy! How can justice ever rectify such a thing?"

The young man did not reply to this question and the Professor turned this attention to him again, ashamed for having allowed the expression of his own feelings to have interrupted his son

"I went round to her room this morning," he was saying, and now his voice began to stumble over his words He had come, no doubt, to something more significant and important than anything he had mentioned so far "I went round to her room this morning Last night she was all right At least, she was all right in her mind, or no worse than one would have expected Well, this morning she was dead I mean that she had killed herself"

He had spoken these last words with the utmost difficulty and now stopped, staring into his father's face with wild eyes His jaws were tightly clenched but could not entirely repress a twitching of the lips The rest of his face was hard, as though frozen

For a moment the Professor felt an impulse to take his son's hand between his two hands and to pat it, or else to smooth back his hair from his forehead, pronouncing at the same time some words of sympathy and condolence, as he might have done on some occasion, many years ago, when his boy had fallen off a bicycle or grazed his knee while climbing a wall. He resisted this impulse and asked gently "And did she leave no message behind for you?"

The young man looked at him gratefully Perhaps he had been afraid of some untoward demonstration of affection, and had dreaded secretly that least element of insincerity which in such a matter would be almost certainly apparent "Yes, she did," he said, and took from his pocket some folded sheets of notepaper But as he was passing these pieces of paper across the table something, whether it was in the touch or sight of them, released his feelings and broke down his careful restraint He let the paper fall on the table, and dropped his head upon his arms, weeping as though he were alone and much younger than he was, a child, in fact, with some certain hope irretrievably and suddenly shattered. The very restraint under which he had kept himself added volume and a kind of shamelessness to his cries, and now the Professor was by his side, as last night he had stood by Jinkerman, patting his back, yet unable to find an entrance through the wall of dismay and of pain that separated him from his own flesh and blood

After some moments his son looked up and said: "It's all right," then relaxed, his head upon his arms He was weeping more quietly and more, as it were, to himself

The Professor thought of the lament which Homer, in the 22nd Book of the Iliad, puts into the mouth of Andromache Were such dignified expressions of grief, he wondered, merely the make-believe of a poet, or were they drawn from real life in societies that were differently organized from anything now existing in the world? For in modern society a sufferer will sin against decency and convention if he alludes to, much more if he expresses, his sufferings. He can expect no audience to listen to his laments or to take up with him a sympathetic chorus To-day the herd will not pause for a weakling, and all grief, in so far as it impairs efficiency, is ranked as weakness Was this stoicism, or was it inhumanity? "O World! O Life! O Time!" the Professor muttered to himself In the centre of his vision he saw with extraordinary clarity the bowed head, straggling hair, and shaking shoulders of his son, and all around was a waste of the chaotic or of the indifferent The boy's body was strong, his mind active and adventurous He was made for love Now he had lost something which could never be recovered It would be impossible to find an argument, however subtle, to prove tñat the damage which had been done to him could ever be made good Not if he were to live for ever, not if he were to grow as wise as Socrates All his dreams might come true, but he would still know that this thing that had happened was not a dream and could never be regarded as such The world, spinning into boundless space, must leave behind it scrawled across time a record of cruelty and senselessness absolutely indelible All these facts the Professor knew, and yet was himself not wholly dejected No blow quite so overwhelming had ever crushed through the inner circle of fortifications that defended his own personality He thought, for instance, of his own wife, and could remember no circumstance that was entirely without charm or graciousness Was he, if he were to say "Such things will happen," more wise or more ignorant, more philosophical or less so, older ot younger than his own son?

His hand picked up the pieces of paper that his son had dropped upon the table He took his spectacles from his pocket, adjusted them on his nose, and while he could still hear the subdued noise of sobbing began to read what the girl had written before she put an end to her life He read as follows

"My dear, criminals and suicides are supposed to be impelled, when they are face to face with their acts, by a desire to justify themselves in the eyes of some impartial witness To me the word "justification"seems to have little meaning—or perhaps a meaning that is too deep for me, for a I through the last hours the old sentence has been recurring in my thoughts, 'In thy sight shall no man livin be justified' 'In whose sight?'

ask myself, or What exactly is demanded?' and I cannot answer my questions

"But I know that what I am writing to you is not 'justification' I want to minimize the pain which I know that you will feel, and I think that I can do so by making plain one or two things

"When you find me dead your first sorrow will seem selfless, but soon you will be inclined to blame me for what will in some way or other appear to you as an act of desertion I am it is true, deserting you and deserting the work that we were doing together

"Then you will, perhaps, be overwhelmed by a feeling of hatred for the young men who made me suffer You may demand' revenge It would be natural Yes, all cruelty is hateful, but it is no more hateful than it always was because it has been applied to me.

"And I must not pretend that it was solely what happened to me last night that has made me end my life After all I am by no means the first woman to have been so treated And there are, perhaps, worse humiliations from which people have still survived

"But I cannot live for what is not as perfect as it can be, and for some time now I have been beginning to suspect that I have, as it were, hopelessly overdrawn my account upon a barren and bankrupt future I have only thought (and that is my weakness) of one thing My one desire has been to live with you in a way that my ambitious dreams described to me as perfect To come to you on absolutely equal terms, as a comrade and a lover—that has been the most important of my dreams since we first met each other

"Now it is true that after last night I feel soiled and outraged I know that for some time you could never embrace me perfectly, because you would always feel pity for me instead of the love that I had imagined But this is not the reason for my suicide Those feelings would, I suppose, pass in the end After all we are not vases

"No, the reason is that I see now, more clearly than I could have imagined possible, that my dreams were all the time false and that, by dreaming them so constantly, I have made myself unfit for life You remember that yesterday, when we were in the wood, I said that I agreed with you that we were unfortunately engaged in war, and that, at such a juncture, love was out of place I thought that I understood what you meant I would submit, though reluctantly, to a postponement of what I still considered as our truest life, the life which, in happier times, we could live together

"Now? see that what I, and I think you too, most desired must not be postponed but finally abandoned Do you remember that I said to you just before your father interrupted us that a few pleasurable sensations, some tender memories were all that we could now give to each other? I was speaking in a kind of cynical way, in spite of my tears But now I see, with horror, that my words were strictly true It is not that what they did to me last night has injured me permanently, has blunted my feelings or filled my mind with hatred It is not that which has made me unfit for love On the contrary, I have begun to feel far more intensely than ever before, and this is just what I cannot bear. I have suddenly realized that what happened to me is happening to some other woman every minute of the day in some part of the world. and worse things than that Children, for instance, are even more defenceless than women, and even minds can be as thoroughly outraged as bodies Do you see what I mean? Such a statement as 'the evil in the world outweighs the good' sounds merely stupid The point is that in the midst of so much evil there can be no good Even to dream of love in such a world is guilty What is needed is a surgeon and, if not that, a destroyer.

"Do not think, my dear, that I am speaking out of bitterness Perhaps if there were more bitterness in me, more indignation, my state would not be so hopeless Say, if you like, that I am hyper-sensitive when I feel all the misery (and the senselessness of it—that is the worst thing) crowding upon me or spread out for miles and miles wherever I look

"Well, what I see I cannot avoid seeing Perhaps a braver person would not see so much Perhaps the horror of the world which I now feel would not be felt if I had approached life in a more scientific spirit But I always looked for happiness I am not a Stoic to fight hopelessly, and in the name of virtue, what I cannot see as anything but a losing battle I wanted nothing but for us to love each other and to work together Ambition should be made of sterner stuff, or else should live in a different world.

"I feel more happy now that I have decided to die, and it is only the thought of your sorrow that gives me any uneasiness You will make a better job of life than I could do You will, I think, not be able to love, but you will fight against some of the evils that have prevented love Do not think that I am acting out of bitterness Even now I do not hate the world. It is simply that I cannot bear it."

The Professor folded the letter carefully and put it back on the table He then pushed it cautiously across the polished mahogany towards his son who was now sitting upright with tousled hair and with an expression that was less strained than it had been before he had been overcome by tears It was quite true, thought the Professor, that at this very moment in thousands of rooms, in thousands of open places, events were taking place which no amount of theological ingenuity could possibly justify "My dear boy," he began in a low and hesitating voice, "I can say nothing to you about the reality of your loss I an unfitted to do so It would be an impertinence. But may I just say this? For myself I can find only one answer that can be made to that letter. It is to use our best energies in making of this terrible world a place in which sensitive and good people may be able to bear to live"

The beginning of a smile came to his son's lips There was a look in his eyes, the Professor thought, of gratitude "I was sure that you would say that," the young man began, "that is the only thing which I too have to believe in Well, I have come to you with a request"

"You may be sure that I will do anything," said the Professor quickly, but his son interrupted him

"Wait," he said. "Let me explain first of all what it is I have come to ask you to arm the workers"

The expression of eager kindness in the Professor's face changed to one of seventy He was, indeed, at first even shocked at the abrupt transition from the tragic story of a private disaster to a proposal for general policy. And the

precise request made was one to which he could never assent
To arm one section of the people, other than the legally constituted forces, and to arm this section against other elements
in the same state! It was impossible, and his son must see it
to be so And yet how was he to meet with a flat denial this
evidently sincere demand, this first effort on his son's part,
after the crushing blow that had fallen upon him, to influence
again the course of life lived by human beings?

His son began to speak again "I am acting," he said,
"unofficially, but with the knowledge of the Central Committee
of our Party"

The ordinary phrases sounded to the Professor more pathetic
than tears. It was as though his son had changed rapidly into
another costume in which, however, his identity was still
apparent Or it was as though this political jargon was in
reality a language with a second meaning, a meaning that
referred to events much closer to the heart than the meetings
of agitators in crowded and smoky rooms? The Professor
could respect emotion and, in his son's words, he respected
rather the echo of the individual loss than the sense of any
proposal that he was likely to make

The young man continued "We have our secret service
organization just as the Government has, and we are convinced
that the Government may be attacked at any moment now,
both from within and from abroad If you yourself have not
received the same information that is a sign that there are
people in the police who are working against you I know
that you will not listen to me if I tell you of our suspicions of
some of your colleagues in the Cabinet; but we are prepared
to put before you, if you like, the evidence on which our
suspicions rest We don't pretend to agree with your policy,
since we believe that it will be impossible to carry out, but we
are willing and anxious to put the whole weight of our movement behind your Government for the specific object of resisting
the invasion from across the frontier and the rising of the
National Legion here—both of which, we are sure, have been
planned to take place shortly

"Perhaps you see now why I began by telling you what has
happened to my friend. Those things are not accidents. they
are part of the deliberate policy of the National Legion. No,
don't smile It is true For my evidence I can appeal to history
and to their own textbooks How then can you give democratic

rights to those who openly declare their intention of destroying democracy? Do you not see that we have two worlds at war, a party of hate and a party of love? And since things are so we are anxious to forget our differences with you, to use all our efforts to establish a common front with your Government for this single aim—the avoidance of bloodshed and the horrors that you can imagine, the preserving of what we, and you too, regard as at least the elements out of which civilization may grow But for us to co-operate fully we insist that the workers should be armed In this way it will be possible for the plebiscite to be taken without any disorders that might be used by our enemies as an excuse for foreign intervention We will give guarantees "

Here the Professor interrupted "My dear boy," he said, "I am afraid that it is useless to continue Do not think that I fail to appreciate your motives, or that I am blind to the dangers which are hanging over us Let me say too that there is much—very much—in the programme of your party with which I am in agreement, whereas to the programme of the National Legion I am entirely opposed But there is one thing more important than my own point of view It is the Idea of Democracy It is the Idea of Justice and Legality I can never arm one faction among my own people against another faction Believe me, my dear boy, that even at this hour persuasion may be proved more powerful than violence. Hatred must be cast out, I assure you, not by hatred but by sympathetic under-standing I agree with you that some members of the National Legion appear to hate everything which you and I regard as deserving of love But for the hatred which they feel we must, in some sense or other, take the responsibility Democracy is not only a theory It is a faith, and the faith is based on the native goodness of man. I, for one, cannot betray that faith I will tell you what I propose to do I am going this morning to see the broadcasting authorities, and shall make arrangements by which I can speak to the whole nation The people will hear, in my own voice and in my own language, the irresistible arguments which must impel them to take their stand behind the Government For, as you will certainly admit, we have only a small minority (though a dangerous one, I grant you) which is in favour of sacrificing our country's independence I shall, naturally, address myself chiefly to the workers, since they constitute the majority of our people, but I think that everyone who is not a traitor will be prepared to support me when I point out."

He was interrupted by the ringing of the telephone bell, and as he picked up the receiver he noticed that once more a look of dismay, like that which he had noticed during his lecture, had settled on his son's face He took up the receiver and put it to his ear As he listened his face became graver After some minutes he replaced the instrument on his table and rose hurriedly to his feet "Dr Tromp," he said, "has been assassinated I must go to the Chancellory at once" He noticed the folded letter that still remained on the table by his son's elbow, and stretched out his hand "Come and see me after I have made my speech," he said "You may be sure that I shall always be ready to listen to you. And you may thank your organization for the support which, in any case, I am sure that they will give me"

He moved rapidly to the door, hardly noticing the look on his son's face, and escorted by the two policemen, who had received instructions to accompany him wherever he went, descended the stairs and made his way to the car that was waiting for him outside the College gates

His son stood at the window and watched the procession through the quadrangle He then picked up the letter and put it in his pocket While he had been advocating a political expedient his face had been animated, but now it was tightened and clenched into the lines of harsh despair

CHAPTER VIII

PREPARATIONS

OUTSIDE the College gates the Professor noticed first of all the cherry tree that he had admired the day before Last night's high wind had now half-stripped the bough of blossom, but the morning was fine, windless, and would soon be warm

Sergeant Jinkerman was waiting by the car, and the Professor invited him to enter it with him so that he might be informed of the'young officer's interview with the Chief of Police and of his views on the general situation. "You have seen Colonel Grimm?" he asked, and Jinkerman nodded his head

"He has promised to make what seem to me the necessary arrangements," he said "Only I wish that I was in charge of them myself"

The Professor observed that Jinkerman was still too inclined to hint as the suspicions which he had of the integrity of the Chief of Police He admired the young man and was grateful to him for his action on the previous night, but he could not permit criticism of a high Government official from a suboidinate. He was about to ask for further information about the pamphlet when Jinkerman spoke again

"You have heard of what happened to your son's girl?" he said.

The Professor pressed his hands tightly together before replying "It is terrible. Terrible."

Jinkerman gave him a quick look in which sympathy was blended with surprise It seemed that he had not expected the father to have been so disturbed by the loss that had befallen the son The Professor continued speaking. "It was most tragic," he said, "and most admirable to see him fighting down the appalling despair which, I know, surrounds him This morning he was literally speaking through his tears when he came to me with a proposal from people whom I imagine must befriends of yours"

"And what answer did you give him?" Jinkerman asked.

"I can do nothing," said the Professor shortly, "that is not strictly in accordance with the Constitution"

The car was passing through the shopping centre, where on the previous day the Professor had been invited to try on a gas mask To-day the streets presented an unusual appearance, for there was double or treble the normal number of police on duty, and in one street alone the Professor noticed three small demonstrations being dispersed.

One of these demonstrations consisted of National Legionaries, fifteen or twenty young men with a banner on which were written the words of the pamphlet which they had distributed earlier "Save your savings," "Down with Anarchy," and "United we stand" The young men looked happy and confident. They were standing smartly to attention while their leader was conversing almost affably with a police officer who was, no doubt, instructing him to lead his procession through the town'by a less crowded thoroughfare

The leader of the second demonstration was no other than

the Rev Furius Webber, who earned a sandwich board on the two sides of which were inscribed the slogans, "Let us be kind" and "No violence, please" He was standing almost by himself on the pavement, his teeth glittering in a smile, while behind him the small company of his followers were being hustled rather roughly into a side street by the police.

The third party of demonstrators seemed to consist entirely of workers from the factories. The men were shabbily dressed, and in such small numbers seemed, from the defiant looks on their faces, ill at ease in this unfamiliar quarter of the town They carried a banner on which was written, "All support the Government," "Freedom, Democracy, Independence" As the car passed them the Professor observed that a fight was on the point of breaking out between the demonstrators and the police, one of whom was attempting to wrest the banner from the hands of the man who held it Around the group stood a considerable number of spectators whose agitated expressions might have denoted sympathy with either of the two parties to the dispute.

Jinkerman leant towards the Professor and touched him on his arm. "If you had eyes," he said in his cold and confident voice, "yoú might see who your real supporters are It is a Whole class whose existence and life you may theorize about but have never understood You talk pedantically of the state as though it were a sum of individuals You have no comprehension of the mass and force represented by these individuals in their collective groups. You do not see that your abstract ideas can nowadays only have meaning for one class, the only class that has nothing to gain from denying them, the only class that is interested in making these abstractions realities You refuse to arm them you refuse to arm your own ideas"

There was so much sincerity in the man's words that the Professor could not be indignant. "Come, come," he said, "you are speaking very confidently, and yet you do not understand my position at all"

Jinkerman threw up his hands in a gesture of impatience "If I was really interested in remaining alive," he said bitterly, "I should have left this country by now."

The Professor looked at him with a smile. "Now, now, my dear fellow," he said, "we must not have any defeatism, you know. By this afternoon I hope to convince you not only that your fears are exaggerated, but that I am perhaps more of a friend to the working-classes than you imagine." And with considerable enthusiasm the Professor outlined his plan foi a public broadcast to be delivered at eleven o'clock that morning He entrusted Jinkerman with the task of making the appropriate arrangements at the Central Radio Station and asked him to report later at the Chancellory when the arrangements were completed To all this Jinkerman listened intently, from time to time nodding his head, but he expressed no enthusiasm for, and little interest in the plan

The car reached the street in which the Chancellory was situated, and here again there was a crowd, though differently composed from the one which, whether venal. or not, had welcomed the Professor on the previous day A dense mass of men and women was standing opposite the Chancellory steps. They were of all classes and ages, and nearly all of them were staring with upturned faces at the blank windows of the big building In almost complete silence they watched the Professor leave his car and mount the steps, and this silence was, to the Professor, even more inspiring than the cheers with which he had been previously greeted. He could feel the tension, understand the bewilderment of those faces He could guess what were the anxious words concerning peace or war which were whispered from one to another And at this crisis in his nation's history he had determined upon giving a clear and unmistakable lead, so that, he fancied, in the future this confused hour would be regarded almost kindly as the proverbial dark one that precedes the dawn

So full was he of these excellent intentions that when he had reached the door of the Chancellory he could not resist the impulse to turn round and wave his hat to the expectant crowd, a gesture most unlike him and only to be explained by the almost feverish exhilaration with which he was accustomed to face any difficulty whether in the field of scholarship or in politics But when he turned round he discovered that behind him were Jinkerman and three or four policemen, all standing close together with the object, no doubt, of screening him "Be quick," Jinkerman whispered, and the Professor remembered, with something of a shock, that according to the information which he had received over the telephone his predecessor in the office of Chancellor had been shot that morning while standing exactly where he was standing now. He passed

quickly inside the building and heard behind him a low sound
from the crowd which reminded him of the noise of a sigh.

The great hall inside the doorway was, after the street, dark
and cool, like a tank for fish The Professor noticed, as he
went up the stairs, the grave faces and respectful bearing of
guards, ushers, and other officials who were on duty Outside
an open door that faced the room in which the Cabinet met
two soldiers with fixed bayonets were standing, and between
them the Professor could see, inside the room, an object resting
on a large armchair and covered with a white sheet This was,
he made no doubt, the body of Dr Tromp, and, taking off his
hat, he stood for perhaps a quarter of a minute gazing into the
room while the two soldiers, with impassive faces, stared past
him into the wall. He then turned to the door opposite, and
going in was immediately greeted by the Chief of Police whom
he found standing as he had been standing yesterday with his
back to the window and with his hands in his pockets.

Colonel Grimm clicked his heels to attention and saluted
when the Professor opened the door. Then, as he shook hands,
his short smile seemed to play about his lips like lightning
"Remarkably fit, remarkably fit," he replied when the Professor
inquired about his health, and indeed his whole bearing was
brisk and buoyant

But what impressed the Professor most about his colleague
was that he seemed in no way perplexed or dismayed by the
situation in which the Government then found itself, and it was
gratifying indeed to find at least one person who remained
confident and who could be trusted, so he imagined, to act with
equability and decision

Colonel Grimm gave a short account of how the ex-Chancellor
had been shot while on the point of entering the Chancellory.
The assassin had not yet been identified, but the police had
arrested all the occupants of the house from which it appeared
that the shot had been fired and were confident that before
many hours had passed they would be able to find either the
murderer or some clue to his whereabouts In Colonel Grimm's
opinion the assassination of Dr Tromp and the attempt on the
Professor's own life were not necessarily the work of the same
organization And in particular he was inclined to doubt the
theory that the National Legion had had any hand in these
acts of terrorism It was true that their papers were full of
attacks on the Government and it was likely that they had been

responsible for the circulation of the pamphlet attacking the Professor's Economic Plan; but these very facts would naturally predispose the Government against them, and it was thus, to Colonel Grimm's way of thinking, most improbable that the Legion should have planned murders which would almost Certainly be attributed to them and which, by arousing the horror of all decent people, could not conceivably further their cause It was true that Vander had been wearing the Legion uniform, but the Chief of Police had found no record of his having been at any time connected with the Legion organization He was inclined to think that the atrocities were the work either of foreign agents or, as a quite possible alternative, of the Reds, who had acted in such a way with the sole object of casting the blame on their enemies Consequently he was redoubling his precautions against both organizations, but had so far received no information that could lead him to suspect that there was, from any quarter, any plan for a *coup d'état*

With the general sense of this analysis the Professor was very well pleased, though he pointed out that there seemed to be absolutely no evidence to suggest that the organization of the extreme Left, whatever their ultimate intentions might be, were at the moment anything but loyal to the Government He informed Colonel Grimm of his own plan for broadcasting to the nation that morning, and assured him that a quarter of an hour at the microphone would be sufficient utterly to discredit the authors of the pamphlet and, in view of the foreign danger, to rally the whole people behind the Government

"Do you propose to broadcast from the Chancellory?" Colonel Grimm asked, smiling as though in approbation of the plan, and the Professor nodded his head

"Yes," he said, "and I have entrusted Sergeant Jinkerman with the task of making the necessary arrangements"

The Chief, of Police smiled again his two smiles "Very good," he said, "I shall give myself, if I may, Professor, the great pleasure of listening in to you from an adjoining room." He paused, and then added in a casual tone of voice, "But what is this I hear about the Commodore and the Trade Union man?"

"A stupid and unnecessary quarrel," the Professor replied "Of course, they will have to confirm their resignations in writing, and I very much doubt whether they will do so. In any case we will, no doubt, be able to persuade them to stick to their posts, though I don't mind telling you, sir, that in my opinion we should do much better without them Still we must, above all, appear before the people as a united and representative Government"

"Precisely," said Colonel Grimm "I agree with you entirely I would suggest, therefore, that we keep this unfortunate affair secret, and even that we deny any rumours that may already have been put about. I say this because the Commodore has already left the country, and as for the Trade Union leader, my officers have so far been unable to find him. I would respectfully suggest that, just at the moment, we cannot afford to allow these facts to be generally known."

You are right," said the Professor. "It is essential that this morning I stand before the people as the head of a united Cabinet This ridiculous quarrel has, it is true, somewhat weakened my position, but the quarrel has nothing whatever to do with the policy of the Government. I do not think, there-fore, that we can reasonably be accused of deceiving the people if we deny any rumours of there having been a crisis in the Government. A crisis, after all, implies a divergence on policy. All that happened has been a stupid display of temper."

Colonel Grimm took a sheet of typewritten paper from his pocket "I am entirely in agreement with you, my dear Chancellor," he said "May I, then, have your written authority for dealing with these rumours? It is not, strictly speaking, necessary, but would assist me possibly with certain editors and even with one or two of my own officers Discipline, you know, is not in these times precisely what it should be!"

He seemed inclined to say more, but the Professor inter-rupted him "Why, certainly," he said "I am not ashamed to put my name to any measure which I authorize." He read rapidly through the words on the paper. It was a statement to the effect that no crisis and no disagreement on policy existed among the Cabinet; that the Chancellor spoke in the name of a united and a confident Government

The Professor signed his name, and blotted the paper. "A deception, if it be one," he said, as he replaced the fountain pen in his pocket, "which is entirely innocent," but he could not escape a slight feeling of distress when he reflected that in the past twenty-four hours he had twice given his assent to the publication of what was not the complete truth.

Somewhat hurriedly he went on to discuss with the Chief of

Police the measures which had been taken to prohibit any further distribution of the pamphlet attacking his economic plan He was informed that while large numbers had certainly been circulated already, the police had that morning confiscated no less than a hundred thousand copies which were still undistributed Colonel Grimm was now inclined to make light of the incident, pointing out that after the broadcast the authors of the pamphlet would be revealed as having deliberately misrepresented the Professor's intentions, and that consequently their work would serve rather to discredit the opposition than to weaken the Government "The only thing," he concluded "which at all alarms me, is the fact that someone or other, either through treachery or through carelessness, must have allowed a copy of your plan to get into the hands of our enemies I was wondering whether perhaps anyone else, apart from the members of the Cabinet, was in possession of a copy"

"Only my economic advisers," said the Professor He thought of the copy which he had given Clara, and, pleased to be accurate, added, "They and a very dear friend of mine No, I prefer to think that it was carelessness, and from what I have seen this morning of two of our colleagues, I should say that either of them is capable of that"

Colonel Grimm smiled "That Trade Union fellow," he said "No brains, I am afraid Or I have seen no evidence of them"

"Very little, certainly," the Professor replied "Indeed it has often surprised me to find that working men who are, so far as I can judge from my own experience, eminently practical and level-headed, should constantly elect as their leaders people who are no better than wind-bags Still the Athenians were just as bad Think of Cleon"

"Exactly," said the Chief of Police "And now, sir, I must leave you to prepare your speech and to attend to your correspondence We can, at all events, be thankful for one thing The situation on the frontier seems definitely easier We have had no more insults from the Ambassador As a matter of fact, I met him quite by chance this morning and he was quite affable Though I am afraid you will find that in his country's press the attacks made on us are as bitter as ever But I still say that, in my opinion, the situation is easier, distinctly easier And we can't expect everything to settle down at once"

"*Solvitur ambulando,*" said the Professor brightly, as Colonel

Grimm made for the door. *"Solvitur ambulando* This news is most gratifying I must say, my dear Colonel, that I have been greatly cheered by our conversation"

"I, too, sir," said the Chief of Police, pausing at the door He went out and left the Professor busy with what he regarded as the most important business of the day, the preparation of his speech

But as he allowed his mind to become free of the urgent preoccupations of the moment, as he contemplated in the recesses of his soul those general principles to which he would appeal when requiring the support of the people for his programme of justice and of legality, his mood of almost reckless confidence began to give place to a more accurate estimation of the forces by which he was opposed He thought now with a kind of horror of Vander's suggestion that, in the course of centuries, the power of reason, so often flaunted, had in these last days lost its appeal He thought, too, of the real force of men and metal which he knew was waiting across the frontier and which, in no calculation, could ever be discounted If he had to deal only with internal unrest, or only with the danger of foreign intervention, his task would not be so heavy If his supporters were more united or his enemies more obvious his course would be plainer In his own mind he saw distinctly and with a kind of love the attractive power of a reason that permeated frontiers and dominated the interests of classes But his sense of immediate obstacles still made him wish that he had had more time, more uninterrupted opportunity to demonstrate logically and irrefutably to each man and woman in the land the justice of the measures which now in the teeth of war and under the threat of assassination he was still proposing. For the first time he began to envisage the possibility of failure; not that he feared that he would be unable in his speech to convince the people of the integrity of the Government, but only because he was beginning to realize the overriding importance to him of time. Suppose that the army massed on the frontier, ready to intervene, should be set in motion before the plebiscite could be held He could see, following from that supposition, a whole train of difficult and even disastrous consequences But Colonel Grimm appeared to believe that the danger from across the frontier was diminishing and the Professor himself knew that, in the present state of international affairs, an invasion would not be attempted unless the invading army could discover some pretext of some apparent plausibility which might seem to justify such an act The Professor was determined that no pretext of any kind must be given to them, and made a note, heavily underlined, to that effect before continuing in the composition of his speech

So he worked for some twenty minutes until his telephone bell rang and he was informed that there was a lady waiting downstairs and asking to be allowed to see the Chancellor on urgent business. It was Clara, and the Professor's face relaxed into a smile as he gave orders for her to be shown immediately to his room., In fact, while he was waiting for her, he began to feel unreasonably but most pleasantly encouraged, as though he were a believer in luck or in providence, as the thought that he was being so visited at such an important juncture of his life by the one person to whom he could most readily turn for sympathy and affection He had much to do that morning He had to interview the Under-Secretary for Foreign Affairs and to arrange a meeting with the two ambassadors representing the powers that might be counted as allies; but all of this business would be better transacted after his speech had been made, and what better preparation for his speech could he have, he asked himself as Clara was being shown into the room, than a few moments' conversation with this upright, beautiful, and understanding woman?

He observed at once that she was either anxious or distressed. Below the dark green hat her face was pale and her lips seemed to have contracted their fullness into a line of red. Particularly he remarked the tawny hair that, escaping from the compression of her hat, hung about her ears; for to-day it seemed lifeless, wilted, like parched plants He had never seen her before unless alight with vivacity or else reflective in a kind of healthy and powerful calm, and now the sight of her without her gaiety and her confidence was to him most pitiful, for he had imagined her to be, in so far as her feelings were concerned, beyond the reach of misfortune.

She stood by the table at which he was sitting, and he rose to kiss her and to squeeze gently her right shoulder-blade with the extended hand of the arm that encircled her body. "What is it my dear?" he asked, and she smiled at him before seating herself in an armchair close to his side, but with her face turned slightly away from him.

"It is nothing very much," she said in a voice that seemed to be trying to recover its usual gaiety "Though I know that I must look a terrible fright Perhaps it is just because I have been worrying about these assassinations"

"You mean the murder of Dr. Tromp," said the Professor. "Yes It is very sad Poor old man. I should think that he can never have injured anyone in this life." He reflected that Clara might be worried about his own safety and added brightly "But I think, my dear, that we now have the situation well in hand If I were a betting man I should be prepared to wager that in a few hours' time the state of the country will be very different from what it is now. At such times very little is needed either to destroy or to restore confidence Well, I am pretty sure that it will be restored. Will you come and see me this evening for dinner (shall we say eight o'clock?) so that we can discuss how right or wrong I have been?"

Clara's face was still grave "Yes," she said, "I will come and see you, but there is one thing which I must ask you first." She paused, and then smiled as though she were introducing unwillingly a subject of small importance "The truth is," she continued, "that I am visiting you almost in the capacity of an ambassador from the enemy."

"Really, my dear," said the Professor "This is most alarming"

Clara smiled again, though somewhat wearily. "I have some friends," she said, "who must have been very slightly implicated in some plot against the Government Please do not ask me their names, because I can assure you that they are very unimportant people."

"Certainly, certainly," said the Professor "Your word is naturally quite sufficient."

"Well," said Clara, "these friends of mine have another friend—I'm afraid this sounds very complicated—another friend who may be, perhaps, a much more dangerous character. He is connected, I rather think, with the National League, and from what my friends say, he was busy last night with some sort of political work. Anyway he has disappeared, and my friends think he may have been arrested So they asked me to come and intercede for him. I suppose that if he has done something bad he will have to remain in prison, but they are really anxious to know where he is and that he is safe. Do you think, my dear, that you could make inquiries? I forgot to mention the man's name. It is Julius Vander"

The Professor started with surprise and then began to speak in a grave voice "I am very sorry," he said, "that you will not be able to take back to your friends any reassuring news" He gave her an account of how Vander had visited him on the previous night and how his attempts at intimidation and at murder had been frustrated by Jinkerman's prompt action

This affair he had intended to keep secret from her since he could guess that she would be disturbed by the thought of such extreme danger so narrowly avoided, and even now, though he took pains to pretend that he himself had been less near to death than had actually been the case she seemed to find the news of his escape almost overpowering She uttered a low moan and let her head fall back against the back of the chair when he had finished his account Her face was so white that he feared a fit of fainting or hysterics, and the sight of her in such obvious distress was even more moving to him than had been her first appearance in the room when he had seen her, for the first time in his life, as a person acutely in need of either protection or assurance

He knelt down beside her chair and took her head between his hands "There, there," he said "It is all over now There will be no more risk of that happening Really I wouldn't have told you, if I'd known—"

She laid a hand across his mouth and began to stroke his moustache with her fingers "I had no idea," she said softly, as though to herself Then she began to cry quietly, and the Professor, who had never seen her before as otherwise than in complete control of her emotions, gently stroked her hair and the material of which her hat was made, whispering words of endearment over her slowly shaking shoulders

There was a knock on the door, and this seemed to act on Clara as a stimulus to regain her self-possession She rose quickly from the chair and went to the window where she stood, with her back to the room; busying herself with a mirror and a powder-puff The Professor went to the door and found that Jinkerman with a party of technicians from the Radio Station had arrived to make the final arrangements for the broadcast Clara, in reply to his invitation to stay and watch the proceedings, said with a smile which seemed to the Professor infinitely pathetic that she would prefer to listen to his speech From her own house So he escorted her downstairs and then returned to supervise the setting of a scene which was to be, he knew, momentous in the fortunes of his country Clara's agitation had endeared her to him all the more, and it was with a subtle sense of sweetness lingering in the back of his mind that he now prepared to demonstrate the strength and fidelity of the Government

CHAPTER IX

THE BROADCAST

As the clocks were striking eleven it seemed, even from the upper room in the Chancellory, as though a hush had fallen upon the city From the windows one might have seen the whole street packed with faces, still eagerly upturned in expectation, although now their attention was directed not so much to the windows themselves as to the black protuberances of loud speakers which had been placed at regular intervals on balconies along the front of the building In other streets, too, the sight would have been the same, while in hundreds of thousands of homes families were gathering around radio sets in large or small rooms, staring at the instruments, whether home-made or expensively manufactured, as though those arrangements of wood, glass, and wire were oracles, gods, or idols

And the Professor himself, as he stood on a hearthrug in the Chancellory, smiling to himself while his mind ran rapidly, like some trained mechanic, over the points that he would make in his speech, could imagine and was sharing in the general excitation The people had been informed merely that at this hour the Chancellor would make a pronouncement of national importance, and so great had been the tension, both political and international, of the preceding months, so startling had been the events of the last twenty-four hours that, no doubt, they were in a state of mind that was ready for the reception of almost any kind of news Wild rumours had already, according to Jinkerman, begun to circulate There were some who supposed that the Professor's speech would be a call to arms others suggested that he had already signed away the country's independence and would that morning attempt to justify what he had done Other speculations concerned a change in the Government or a total suppression of the parties of the Left, and some, no doubt owing to the influence of the pamphlet, would have it that the Professor intended to proclaim the dictatorship of the proletariat On such an audience, nervous with expectation and surmise, the Professor could estimate how powerful sn effect would be made by any words which were clear, authoritative, and reassuring.

He had often in the past addressed large numbers of listeners through the microphone and indeed preferred this method of oratory to any other; for, as he would often say, when the person of the speaker was invisible all inessentials and vulgarities were removed and the path of communication from mind to mind was clear. On the one hand the speaker could not bolster up a bad argument by a display of histrionics, and on the other hand the audience were not as a rule subject to those irrational storms of irrelevant emotion that so often overwhelm people when they are gathered together under one roof in a public meeting The Professor himself, moreover, was exceptionally well equipped as a radio orator The tones of his voice suggested not only firmness but also gentleness and a kind of charm, so that he could both convince and reassure. He was, therefore, peculiarly well adapted for dealing with the present situation and it was, no doubt, his own knowledge of his own powers that had kept him even to this eleventh hour confident, unembarrassed, and secure.

Jinkerman had left the room, since he regarded it as still important that the approaches to the Chancellory and even the passages within the building should be guarded by the police under his command. The Professor was now left alone with the chief announcer from the Central Radio Station, a middle-aged man, tall, and with almost excessively polite manners, who had arrived in full morning dress, carrying in one hand a carefully brushed top hat and in the other a malacca cane with a large silver knob as handle. He, alone of all those whom the Professor had met that morning, seemed entirely indifferent to recent political events and to the general danger.

In the few minutes during which they had been waiting for the clocks to strike, he had been speaking in his cultivated and deliberate voice, of the arguments for and against the use of perfume by gentlemen, and now he was beginning a discourse on the qualities required of a radio announcer. "Above all," he was saying, "a good presence is essential" But when the clocks began to strike he went quickly to the microphone on the Professor's desk and, turning to him while he was making the necessary adjustments, said: "As soon as I have announced your name, will you be so good, sir, as to take your place in this chair? A decent, but not too long an interval should elapse after my last words And may I beg you, sir, when you have finished, to vacate the chair immediately, so that I may at once announce the sporting news? And now, sir, silence, if you please" He then seated himself in front of the microphone, straightened his tie, smoothed his hair with the palms of both hands and, in a voice of becoming gravity, began to speak "This is the Central Radio Station. We are taking you over to the Chancellory to hear a statement of national importance from the Chancellor" He then closed his eyes and, holding his left hand in front of him, began to flick out the fingers one by one as though he were counting When he had reached the thumb, or the number five, he opened his eyes and said, in a somewhat louder voice, "The Chancellor" He rose quickly from his place and, looking severely at the Professor, with a sweeping gesture of the hand invited him to be seated, as though he were introducing a fortunate neophyte to the performance of some not unimportant part of a ritual. The Professor cleared his throat, and at once the announcer pressed his extended fore-finger against his lips, raising his eyes to the ceiling with an expression of face that might seem to denote either horror or adoration. The Professor gave him a stern look from beneath his eyebrows, then seated himself before the microphone and began to speak.

He spoke in the cool and level voice that he was used to employ in a lecture room, a voice of transparent sincerity whose tones seemed to declare the confidence born of knowledge and the gentleness that springs from a deep humanity "Fellow-countrymen," he began, "I am speaking to you at this very critical time for three reasons First to declare and to submit to your approval the faith that I, and the whole Government, and I think the vast majority of my listeners have in the principles and in the ideals of democracy Secondly I wish perfectly frankly to describe to you the dangers which at this moment threaten not only our democratic institutions but our very independence as a nation I shall call upon you to stand firm, to stand united, With the assurance that by so doing we shall preserve our own freedom and be also, as we have been so often in the past, an example to the world And thirdly I shall do what may not be and I hope is not necessary. I shall expose what I am quite sure was a deliberate and calculated misrepresentation of my policy I refer to a pamphlet that was circulated in large numbers last night You will be convinced, I am certain, that the authors of that pamphlet have shown themselves indifferent not only to the truth, but to the highest interests of the state.

"Let me begin with my first point. What do we mean by democracy? I ask the question because it is a good thing from time to time to remind ourselves that democracy, so far from being, as some extremists assert, a decadent and outworn system of government, is in fact the most brilliant of man's ideals, an ideal that, pointing as it does farther than we can see into the future, can never be outworn, never be, if properly understood, anything but inspiring Men throughout the ages have given their blood, their brains, their total energies to the carrying into practice of this splendid, enduring, and still revolutionary creed I like to think of us as standing to-day in sight of the peaks at which they have aimed and towards which they have led us Let us never, fellow-countrymen, think of descending again into the valleys, into the darkness of superstition, of intolerance, of tyranny And even though it is true that our goal has not yet been reached, let us above all refuse to listen to those who, from a lack of spirit or of understanding, would have us believe that it is either unattainable or not worth the trouble to attain

"Now, what are the principles of this faith that we hold? The first of them is this We solemnly affirm that in our state every citizen, without exception and irrespective of age or sex or occupation or wealth, should have an absolutely equal voice in the conduct of government What a splendid and far-reaching affirmation, my friends! May I ask you for a moment to reflect on some of the views of human nature which are involved in or implied by such a statement?

"A believer in democracy must, if he is to be logical, admit the unique value of each individual. He will not attempt to deny the great differences which exist between one person and another whether in inherited ability or in the advantages of environment, but he will and must maintain that, over-riding all these differences, is the simple fact of man's unity with man within a community. He Will maintain, also that our community is a human community. We are organized not only for the doing of necessary work, but are combined in cities, are civilized And civilization is more than the efficient use of tools It means, when civilization is democratic, the voluntary co-operation of citizens in search of the good life, of the fullest possible satisfaction, not for a single man or for a few individuals, but for everyone For it is our belief that no man's happiness can be founded on another's misery and that, in an authoritarian state, the tyrant himself is no better than a slave He who does not respect his fellow men cannot respect himself, but to a democrat all men, whatever their inequalities in nature or in status, are equally unique and equally to be respected

"Such statements will seem to some of you paradoxical, and to some, I am afraid, almost hypocritical The workman, for instance, who at the present moment may be in danger of losing his job, will perhaps be saying to himself, 'What is the good of this talk of unique value, of equality in one state, when so obviously some men have uninterrupted security and others are in constant and hazardous dependence on them ?'

"Now that is a question which cannot be set aside, which must be answered And may I say that I regard it as the chief duty of my Government to find an answer, not merely logical and theoretical, but practical, to just this question?

"Fellow-countrymen, I shall not attempt to deny that at present democracy, though admirably complete and consistent as an ideal, is an ideal that is still imperfectly realized This was inevitable The reason is quite simple In the past human societies have not possessed the necessary technique to ensure either leisure or wealth to more than a very small proportion of the community And so while the best minds have always proclaimed that by the laws of God and of Nature all men are equal and free, the necessities of production, the laws of Man have been in conflict with these higher principles But to-day the scientist has made practicable the philosopher's dream To-day there is nothing but prejudice and inertia that prevents us from carrying the principles of democracy immensely farther forward than they have ever been carried before For this triumphant advance the material conditions are already here What else is needed? First of all, peace My Government will, as I shall soon explain to you, secure peace Secondly, discipline; I mean self-discipline, the cheerful and ready obedience of the whole people to the people's laws, to the people's will. Thirdly, a quality most difficult to define. I might perhaps call it 'fair play,' but a better term I think would be 'good will.' In peace, my friends, with discipline and with good will let us go forward as a united, proud, and happy people into a future that, if we will have it so, can become the most splendid age in the history of mankind."

The Professor paused and licked his lips. He could hear in the distance, from the streets, the confused noise of shouting The radio announcer was sitting in an armchair, reading a comic paper which he must have brought with him in his pocket Glancing at his notes, the Professor was about to continue when the door swung open and Jinkerman, with a face most unnaturally pale, entered the room. The announcer at once sprang to his feet and, pressing his finger to his mouth, advanced towards the policeman with, a curiously undulating gait, and making a low hissing noise like some large snake aroused to repel an intruder

Jinkerman took no notice of him, but coming close to the Professor said, "I am afraid, sir, that the game is up" The Professor had covered the microphone with his hand and was looking at Jinkerman in amazement and anger The announcer, with an expression of panic on his face, had thrown his arms loosely round Jinkerman's waist and was clinging to him as a suppliant might embrace some holy image Jinkerman spoke again. "It's no use," he said, pointing to the microphone, "no one can hear a word that you're saying"

The announcer relinquished his hold on the policeman and hurriedly began to examine the instrument through which the Professor had been speaking Only a short inspection was needed. He straightened his back and, with a distraught air, began to run his fingers through his thin hair that now rose like a crest from his polished head "A technical defect! A technical defect!" he muttered "Oh, sir! I could die of shame."

"Technical defect be damned!" said Jinkerman, and now for the first time the Professor observed how extreme was the agitation under which the young man laboured. "This is the story briefly The Chief of Police, with National Legionaries, has occupied the Radio Station and is at present proclaiming himself Chancellor"

The Professor's trained mind was unable for the moment to grasp the meaning of the words "What!" he said. "No. It is impossible You must be dreaming"

There was a radio set in the corner of the room Jinkerman went to it and switched it on. "Dreaming!" he said, "I wish I were"

They heard the low humming of the radio set, then, spoken in a clear unemotional voice, the conclusion of a sentence whose meaning was indistinct The voice was, without question, that of the Chief of Police The Professor let his head sink between the palms of his hands They listened, the reception being remarkably, almost unnaturally, clear

"And so you see," Colonel Grimm was saying, "there was only one course open to me In view of the very grave disorders which have been planned by some of the Chancellor's supporters and which were timed to start at noon to-day I have had to take emergency measures I have had to ask for the assistance of troops from across the frontier I am very glad to say that my request has been acceded to, and I think that we must all be grateful to that mighty country which is our neighbour for helping us at this time to retain our liberty, our lives, and our property Let me repeat that there is no question of sacrificing our country's independence I ask you to consider the soldiers who will very soon be among you not as soldiers but as police-men, as guardians of law and order. It has been a very near thing, my friends An hour or two more and revolution might have reared its ugly head in our back streets and in our principal thoroughfares Bitterness and class war might, in their can-kerous growth, have imperilled our very lives

"Civil war is a very terrible thing. It sets sons against fathers, householders against their neighbours It opens the door to irreligion, the breaking of contracts, anarchy Well, we have avoided civil war. I have enrolled several thousand National Legionaries to act as special constables, and in a very short time our friends from across the frontier will be among us, not, I repeat, as aliens, but as deliverers Let irresponsible elements beware of any attempt to confuse the present issue The anti-revolutionary front is united, solid, and kindly, but will be, if challenged, ruthless Any attempt to hinder the auxiliary police in the performance of their legitimate duties will be dealt with severely The police are authorized, during the next few days, to use their firearms when and where it may be necessary to do so

"One last word Many of you will be wondering how it has come about that the Chancellor could have allowed himself to become involved in a plot against the very constitution of the state of which he was the head, and a plot which is, as I have described to you, so notably treacherous, terrible, and malig-nant. The Chancellor is, as we all know, a clever man Well,

I personally have not much use for that kind of cleverness, and I think that it is a sound instinct which makes ordinary fellows rather distrust the intellectual I will go farther and say that in most cases the intellectual will be found to be a foreigner

"Now it will take some days before I can produce in the public court the mass of evidence which I have of the organized incendiarism, terrorism, looting of banks, poisoning of reservoirs, commumzation of women (yes! even that), which had been planned by the Professor and his supporters But I have in my hand now, and can produce at any moment a document signed by his own hand and instructing me to conceal the fact that two of his colleagues, the Minister for War and the Representative of the Orthodox Trade Unions, have already left the cabinet, so great was their disgust when they began ever so slightly to suspect (for I know that they had no complete knowledge) in what direction the Professor was going The resignation of these two Ministers does great credit both to the Ministers themselves and to the organizations which they represent Let the army and those loyal workers who have followed the wise leadership of Mr Tubb be proud of the fact that their Minister and their leader, fine fellows and good comrades, have so early dissociated themselves from the nefarious activities of a Chancellor who has succeeded, I admit it, in hoodwinking many of the rest of us right up to the last moment And if there are still any left who, in the face of overwhelming evidence, will still, from a kind of diseased and sentimental loyalty, attempt to make excuses for the Chancellor, let me ask them this question Is it the act of a democrat, is it the act of an honest man to instruct the Chief of Police to withhold essential information from the public?

"Finally let me appeal for calm and discipline I am a simple enough person myself, no statesman, but merely interested in keeping law and order. The interim government which I have proclaimed has only one object—to save your wives and children, your homes, your little gardens, your hard-won possessions from the horror of revolution and anarchy Just so soon as it is possible I shall resign my trust into the people's hands But for the moment, let there be no mistake about it, the law is going to be enforced strictly and impartially. Disturbers of the peace, revolutionaries, men who are for setting neighbour against neighbour, had better beware But peaceable, decent people, people who are prepared to co-operate with the police and to welcome our deliverers from across the frontier have nothing, nothing whatever; to fear The Interim Government offers you three things, Peace, Discipline, and absolutely fair play"

Jinkerman switched off the radio and looked at the Professor as though he were about to ask him a question. The announcer was standing at the door, holding his hat in one hand, while with the other he was straightening his tie. "I think," he was saying, "if you will excuse me," but as no one paid any attention to him, he quietly opened the door and slipped out

The Professor raised his head from between his hands His face was pale and his eyes were ghttering, his tightly shut mouth may have indicated an effort to repress any untimely expression of his horror and of his disgust "If I could obtain a hearing," he said to Jinkerman, "or could have it announced that I have appointed you Chief of Police instead of Colonel Grimm, how many of the police would follow you ?"

"In ordinary times," said Jinkerman, "nearly the whole force To-day hardly anyone Were you not listening? Did you not hear about the troops? No, there are not many martyrs among the police" He must have noticed the growing dismay that was evident in the Professor's face, for he added "I am sorry for you, Professor You threw away your last chance when you refused your son's request Now there is nothmg for it but to run away"

The Professor turned on him and startled him by speaking in a voice that was several tones higher than usual and that expressed a state of agitation that seemed entirely out of keeping with the scholar's character. "You mean," he said, "that I should have put myself at the head of revolutionaries in order to avoid being accused of having done so."

"Precisely," said Jinkerman "Then there would have been no bloodshed. But you would not arm your own ideas. Now we shall have to run for it"

The Professor looked at him closely and with sympathy He saw that behind Jinkerman's cool and level voice lay the same bitterness of dismay and disappointment that he himself felt. "No," he said, "if we cannot resist, at least I shall stand my ground, and meet my accusers," and, with a gesture that seemed to indicate desperation rather than confidence, he rose quickly to his feet and crossed to room the French windows that opened on to the balcony overlooking the street. "It's no good," Jinkerman said. "It would be better not to show your-self," but he was not to be deterred Opening the window he stepped on to the balcony and looked down upon the dense crowds that still packed the street He raised his hand and opened his mouth as though about to speak

His appearance, by its very suddenness, seemed to have shocked the crowd into silence and immobility The Professor had time to enunciate the word "Fellow-countrymen!" and then, as though at the signal of some unseen conductor, the crowd altogether began to vociferate with shouts, howls, yells, boos, hisses, and screams And in addition to the turmoil of voices there was a rapid and growing agitation of faces and limbs Fists were shaken, umbrellas and walking sticks bran-dished in the air, arms waved, faces contorted with passionate and unreflecting feeling He saw the crowd as he had seen it the day before when it had surged against the police barrier determined to lynch a man assumed to be an assassin. He had calmed it then, but then he had been held in honour and was believed to have been the victim of a dastardly attack To-day not only was the fury of the mob much more intense but, more important, it was directed against himself. For some moments the Professor stood motionless with his arm raised, claiming a hearing At first, in addition to a natural and understandable feeling of fear, he had felt horror and disgust at the sight of such an unchained and brutish convulsion of human nature Now, and for a few moments, he could feel nothing but pity "Fellow-countrymen!" he said again in a low voice which he must have known to be quite inaudible "O Love, O Love ?"

Someone had thrown a bowler hat which rebounded from the base of the balcony The Professor smiled, but the next moment a brick whizzed close by his head and crashed into the room behind He took a step forward, lowered his hands and resting them on the balcony as he leaned towards the crowd below. The shouting and screaming increased There was a perceptible motion as though the mass of people were attracted to him by some force of gravity And yet he was more like a piece of meat in front of beasts than a moon or sun that could influence the tides A bullet clipped a fragment of stone from the balcony by his right hand. Then Jinkerman came from behind and dragged him back into the room "You will do no one any good by having yourself killed," he said. "Come, we must get away from here "

The Professor stood, supporting himself with one hand on the table He felt weak and limp, as though suddenly thrown upon his own resources in some completely unknown and unimagined situation, as though up to now the very fury and hostility of the crowd had communicated strength to him, as though he had been sharing in some mystery and was now banished from the rite He looked blankly at Jinkerman and suffered himself to be taken by the arm and led from the room

In the corridor there were still some policemen on duty and these, so Jinkerman informed him, were trustworthy men of his own detachment They were clearly aware of what had happened but they saluted when they saw the Professor, and one elderly constable actually stopped him, and with tears in his eyes, shook his hand This action seemed to restore the Professor to himself He pressed the old fellow's hand warmly and now began to reflect on what might be the possibilities of resisting the invaders and the traitors from within if he should be able to escape to one or other of the provincial towns at a greater distance from the frontier. But even as he began to contemplate the duty of resistance he envisaged clearly what must be taking place at that very moment, the long procession of troops pouring, unresisted, across the frontier on the invitation of one man and of one small party which had usurped the powers of government by treachery, terrorism, and lying, and which would use its power to persecute, to stifle, and to corrupt The lines of his mouth stiffened, for he had resolved that whatever might happen he would never acquiesce

They had reached a back entrance to the Chancellory buildings, a small door which in the past had been used only for the reception of coal and wine, which from this point could most easily be transferred to the cellars Jinkerman opened this door carefully and peered out into a deserted alley They stepped outside and, as they went cautiously forward, Jinkerman began to explain his plans He proposed to take the Professor to his own father's house, a small cobbler's shop not far from where they were The Professor was to remain there until it was dark and by that time, Jinkerman hoped, arrangements could be made by which they could escape from the town

"You are very kind," the Professor said, as though he were accepting an invitation to some party, and they quickened their steps, for they could hear increasingly loud the angry noise of the mob and guessed that long before long an attempt would be made to have the Chancellory surrounded

"I will get in touch with your son, too," Jinkerman said "I am afraid he will be on the Legion lists and therefore in danger"

The Professor nodded his head. Lists, he thought, proscriptions a return to the savageries of Sulla, of the massacres in which perished the great orator, Cicero But the historical parallels failed to stir his mind: the actual process of life differed too remarkably from recorded history, and no imaginative insight could bridge the gulf between the living and the dead

They had come to the end of the alley and had now to cross a street which they could hardly hope to find empty "Keep at my side," said Jinkerman said, "and don't look about you too much If by any chance we should get separated here is the address." He scribbled a few words on a piece of paper and put it into the Professor's hand The Professor was thinking of Clara His friends, he saw, were in danger and she would most certainly be counted among them He hesitated to ask Jinkerman to run still more risks when, so far as he could see, it was only the man's patriotism and goodness of heart that had prevented him already from making his escape yet he knew that without Clara he himself would never seek safety "There is one other person," he began and, as Jinkerman listened intently, he gave him Clara's name and address "I'll do what I can," he said when the Professor had finished He seemed quite unaffected by the thought of fresh responsibilities or further danger, and the Professor took his hand and pressed it before they stepped together into the street

They could see at once that they were fortunate in not having delayed longer In front of them the street was almost deserted, but some fifty yards away a crowd, amongst which were conspicuous the banners of the National Legion, was making its way towards them They walked sedately across the open space and had almost reached the other side when they heard a cry behind them "There he goes! There he goes! After him; boys!"

They turned their heads and saw that they had been recognized by a boy, fifteen or sixteen years old, a seller of ice creams, who, together with some of his friends, was standing by his bicycle on the pavement All the young boys together began to take up the cry and for the moment the Professor thought not so much of his danger as of the strangeness of a situation in which boys, for an afternoon's sport, with no knowledge whatever of the rights or wrongs of the case, were ready to pursue him as if he were a rabbit or a cat Jinkerman had began to run, and the Professor followed close after him. They reached a side street, turned off it down another, and came to a place where a narrow passage opened in the walls of a building Here they stopped still, hoping that they had eluded their-pursuers, but in a moment the boy who had first seen them, and who, on his bicycle, had outstripped the others, came into sight round the corner. His face was flushed and expressed nothing but enjoyment in the pursuit Wildly hallooing he swept past the alley-way in which Jinkerman and the Professor were hiding Jinkerman smiled, replaced a revolver in his holster, and led the Professor on to his father's house

CHAPTER X

THE COBBLER

THE Professor was sitting in a space so small as to suggest that what now did duty for a sitting-room must have been designed in the first place as a closet or cupboard Two chairs, hard and uncomfortable in spite of their torn upholstery, and a small table were all the furniture The door, when opened half way, struck against the arm of the chair in which he was sitting, so that he had to climb from the passage into his present position No carpet covered the rotting boards of the floor, but in front of the minute fireplace was a small rug on which a cat was sitting upright, and beyond the fireplace was another chair from which an old man, Jinkerman's father, was surveying the Professor through the thick glass of spectacles

The transition from study and Chancellory to this bare place, from his status of authority to his present situation as a hunted refugee, had been so quick and sudden that for some moments the Professor had gratified some portion of his mind by allowing himself to wonder whether what he saw now and what he remembered of the last few hours were not the effects of illusion, whether for some time now he had been not awake, but dreaming The strangeness of his position, confined in so narrow a space and face to face with this old man who, by the immobility of his head and eyes, reminded the Professor of an owl, seemed to

imply that the events immediately past must have been equally
strange, equally unreal He thought of the visit which he had
received that morning from Clara, and now the conduct and
the appearance of Clara herself on that occasion appeared to
him as too unusual and fantastic to have been true. For
actuality his memory returned to days before he accepted the
position of Chancellor, wanderings on moors or papers read
by a subdued light to small audiences on such subjects as the
Arcado-Cypnot dialect Then he seemed to hear with a
startling intensity the half of a sentence spoken over the radio
by the Chief of Police. He was convinced immediately, not so
much of his danger as of his despair; and shifting his position
he rubbed his hand backwards and forwards across his forehead
It was the advance of civilization, the age of tolerance, the
Eonomic Plan that now were dreamlike For he knew that he
was now deprived of all power to intervene, that it would be
unwise for him even to set foot in the streets, and that he had
nothing to do but wait for Jinkerman's return in the hope that
this officer would be able to save from the general wreckage
two individuals who were dear to him

He was immediately startled by an utterance from the old
man who sat facing him In a low but remarkably clear and
confident voice, as though he were making a pronouncement of
general interest, the old man had said: "Enter not into judgment with Thy servant, O Lord For in Thy sight shall no man
living be justified"

The Professor looked wearily across the fireplace at Jinkerman's father He saw he was being regarded intently by those
unblinking eyes which had reminded him of an owl's eyes but
which now, behind the thick lenses of spectacles, seemed less
vivid, presenting, indeed, a drowned appearance like pebbles
seen at the bottom of a pool The lower part of the elder
Jinkerman's body was hidden by a blanket which he had wrapped
about his knees Indeed the Professor had thought, when he
had first climbed into the room, that he was being presented to
a sick man Even now the greater part of his body seemed lifeless, for his legs were hidden and his thin hands motionless,
like abandoned things, on the arms of his chair But the posture
of the head, thrust forward from between the shoulders, was
hawk-like and it might have been deduced that the eyes too,
behind the lenses, were vigorous and penetrating. The Professor was, at this time, more ready to receive sympathy than

instruction, and it was the desire to instruct that was suggested to his mind by the old man's quotation from the scriptures He remembered suddenly that some of the words which he had just heard had appeared in the letter written by his son's friend who had killed herself that morning, and his expression of severity changed into one of interest Then he reflected that the old man, for all he knew, had both heard and believed the Chief of Police Perhaps he was under the impression that the Professor had in reality planned a movement for anarchy and revolution, and perhaps the biblical quotation had been intended to assure him that, black as his conduct might have been, some excuse for it could be found in the general wickedness of mankind

The Professor smiled and said, "I hope, sir, that you do not imagine that you are harbouring a revolutionary I trust that you did not believe what was said about me over the radio" He ceased speaking suddenly, for it had occurred to him how ridiculous was his present situation He had planned logically to enlighten a whole country as to the nature of his ideals, and no one had heard a word Now he was reduced to an attempt to explain to an old cobbler no subject of general importance, but simply the fact of his own integrity.

The old man spoke again in his quiet voice that was made emphatic by the clanty and distinctness with which he enunciated his words "Of course," he said, "Prealized at once that there was little or no truth in what was said by the Chief of Police"

The Professor was not aware that there was a note almost of accusation in the old man's voice The mention of the Chief of Police had caused him to imagine what must already have been the appearance of the streets—the bands of marching Legionaries now vested with the legal power to persecute and destroy their enemies "He has much to answer for," he said gravely

The old man leant farther forward in his chair "I, on the other hand," he said, "am more inclined to regard you as being chiefly responsible for what has happened and what will happen"

The Professor threw out his hand in a gesture of impatience It seemed that, at this crisis of his life, he had become what he had never been in the past, resentful of criticism But in a moment his hand relaxed and he looked gravely at the elder Jinkerman "No doubt," he said, "you agree with your son, and would have had me meet violence by violence, revolution by revplution I could never do myself what I am most disgusted to see done by my opponents But I should have been more vigilant, I know it. More vigilant "

"I do not see," said the old man, "how more vigilance on your part would have saved you, and I myself could not bear to be a party to any kind of violence What I accuse you of is your indifference to the fact of the damnation of the soul."

"Yes," said the Professor abruptly He was thinking of what might have been achieved if, from the very beginning, he had insisted on the resignation of Colonel Grimm His mind then took in the precise words used by the old man "I beg your pardon," he said "I do not quite follow your meaning"

"I fear," said the old man, "that so far from understanding my meaning, you may regard me, simply because I have alluded to the problem, as a man whose intellect is less correctly developed than your own." He spoke now, as before, as though he were stating simple and incontrovertible facts, and there was not hostility, rather the reverse, in the tones of his voice

It was, perhaps, the contradiction between the closeness and squalor of the room and the strangely crystalline quality of the old man's voice that made the Professor feel still uneasy, as though he were being interrogated in a dream "I can assure you," he replied, "that such a suspicion would be quite unjustified No doubt our views on many subjects differ Perhaps on some of these subjects I am better qualified to speak than you are, on others, no doubt, you will have the advantage over me All men, I think, have something to learn from and something to teach others" He smiled, as though he had made some witty or charming remark, but not a muscle of the old man's face moved. His eyes still shone, as though removed to a great distance, behind the thick lenses of his spectacles

"My son," he said, "because I believe in Our Saviour accuses me of indifference You, I think, have no faith Yet what callousness and indifference are revealed by the words which you have just spoken! For what is it that you mean? Will you allow a fellow creature to hold a wrong or a mistaken idea? Can you easily and lightly support the knowledge that other men are on matters of vital importance less well informed than yourself? Or are you uncertain, perhaps, as to whether you yourself are well informed? Worse still, are you not in some danger of actually admiring the state of uncertainty? And yet you have had in your care the precious souls of men Do you not love them?"

The Professor was, for the moment, nonplussed by so unusual an appeal He made no reply and the old man, after having waited for him to speak, continued, "I ask the question," he said, "because I can see that it is a form of love which animates my son and even his opponents My son would, I am afraid, actually kill, if it should be necessary, a fellow man in order to establish conditions which he believes would make the majority of his fellows more wise, more beautiful, happier, and more lovable Some of his opponents, too, aim, however mistakenly, at a kind of comradeship in discipline which, even though it may be manifestly imperfect, does at least recognize the anxiety which brother must feel for brother and for himself You, I think, are alone in isolating man from man, in forcing all, friend and enemy alike, on to their-own resources, in withdrawing yourself, in arrogating to yourself, a mere man, a detachment of which only God is capable and which God, as Our Saviour has told us, does not choose. Do you wonder, then, that when I see your arrogance, your callousness, your shrinking from the world, and, worse than these, your complacency, I ask you how it is that you have forgotten the damnation of souls?"

"I am afraid," the Professor began, "that our religious views do not exactly coincide But when I say that I am content to hold my own view and to allow you to hold yours, does it follow that I am indifferent to you as a human being? May it not be that I respect you so much that I am reluctant to force upon you anything which you will not voluntarily accept? Is not self-government within the soul, just as within the state, a worthy ideal? I believe that the world and human nature are fundamentally good, and that it is interference that is the cause of distortion Nor do I think that you are entirely fair to me when you accuse me of callousness. It is true that a professional scholar is, by the very nature of his work, cut off from the day-to-day activities of the majority of his fellow countrymen, but I may say that all through my life I have been interested in politics and much of my tune during the last few years has been taken up in the production of an economic plan which, I am convinced, would do away entirely with poverty and would go a long way towards preventing war I think you will agree with me that poverty and war are the chief scourges of this generation"

Once more he felt how unnecessary and ineffective were his words A habit of precision rather than any real desire to convince had led him into making thesé explanations He observed that though old Jinkerman had listened intently to his speech, the expression of his face had not changed "On the contrary," he said, "I believe that you and your philosophy are in the long run more dangerous and devastating than either war or póverty"

"Come, come?" said the Professor sharply "I do not think that any system of religious beliefs can lead you to that conclusion You will hardly pretend that I have shown either in my life or in my theories a desire to injure a single human being" He looked with some impatience at the old man, being at the same time angry with himself for having acquiesced in this cross-examination and so having been compelled to boast of his single-mindedness and glorify his efforts at social amelioration, all of which, as he now saw clearly, had been, in fact, frustrated Again his mind went back to the scenes which no doubt were at this very moment being enacted in the streets that, from the seclusion of this pent-in place, seemed remote, although still more real than the close atmosphere in which he was arguing with the religious cobbler For in this narrow space the very springs of his intellect and his tolerance seemed to be drying up He had no wish to continue the discussion, was indeed prepared to admit, in the general ruin of his hopes, that he had miscalculated, that he lacked complete certainty He was particularly irritated now by what at first had rather charmed him, the clear and confident tones of the elder Jinkerman's voice

The old man now moved one of the hands that had lain like dead fishes on the arms of his chair. He leant forward and touched the Professor's knee "Please do not think," he said, "that I am attempting to judge you" He smiled for the first time and the Professor observed that this slow movement of the lips, while it indicated no concession, revealed a kind of tenderness that he would not have expected to find in the old man

He smiled himself and replied: "I must confess that your words seemed to me to imply not only judgment but condemnation."

The smile on the old man's lips at once contracted. "You believe the world is good," he said, "and in some respects, I suppose, it has been good to you You have been surrounded

by the writings of dead poets and, by enjoying them, must have
come to believe that your life was valuable because it was often
pleasant I can well understand what exquisite moments of
delight you must have received from perhaps a line or two of
poetry I, in my youth, have had the same feelings aroused by
poetry although I, no doubt, am much less able than you are
to appreciate its finer points, also by sudden glimpses of
scenery or the sight of the bodies of men or animals in motion
Such pleasures, if they are numerous enough, may easily delude
a person into the belief that the world is as kind as a mother or
else something fascinating to inspect, like a brightly coloured
map. But it is a fact that the world is not removed from us in
this way We are ourselves the world and parts of its working,
and our own hearts are desperately wicked. And when I say
the world I mean the world that is now alive, not the rarefied
essence of what is most precious among the dead

"May I ask you now how you have judged this world?
Is it not chiefly from books and from the men and women who
have had sufficient money to buy and leisure to read them?
There is, I am sure, very much that is gracious in the lives of
such people, but there can be no love and no terror of damnation How have you judged our cities? Has it not been largely
from their art galleries and their architecture? How have you
regarded the world of nature? Have not your views been
formed as a result of occasional visits to selected beauty spots
or to places that in your mind are sanctified by the memories or
monuments of antiquity?

"It was not my choice, but only the will of God that plunged
me among the living, and so I came to look even on nature with
different eyes Charm, sublimity, and grace are the adjectives
which you apply to scenery I see everywhere on the face of
nature the struggle of good and evil Have you given as much
attention to the weasel and the octopus as you have bestowed
on the horse and the gazelle? Has it occured to you that
desolation is as fit a word as sublimity for either the desert or
the sea? How can you love the shade if you have never feared
the sun? There is no love without fear

"But we are discussing, are we not, the world of men And
here, if I can enlighten you, it is not through any supenoi
intelligence but because I have been a great sinner and have
recognized the desperate peril of my soul "

He paused, and the Professor began to feel still more fully

that the scene in which he was taking part was more akin to his dreaming than to his waking life The extraordinary sharpness and clarity of old Jinkerman's enunciation made his words seem like glittering things at a distance From the bottom of a well, the Professor reflected, stars can be seen in daylight. He had become interested in what the old man was saying, and yet a lethargy was spread over his mind so that he hardly troubled to examine any weak points there might be in the argument to which he was listening or to react as he would normally have done to what seemed to be an attack upon his dearest ideals "Please continue," he said politely, "I am quite sure that you must have had experiences which have been extremely enlightening."

"Pain, evil, poverty, complete frustration," said the old man "are not all that is required before a man can know that God is love and can understand the extreme dangers to which his soul is exposed. There is something else needed, something which has always been, I am afraid, very far from your experience It is necessary to know that one is a part of the living world. I was born into that world, and so could hardly escape the knowledge When I say the living world I mean the world of men and women who work consciously in order to live, in order to obtain their food; those, too, who live for themselves in the sense that they are no man's master. No complete philosophical detachment is possible among those who are always employed by others and who know that the food which they eat can only come to them by the labour of their own hands That philosophical detachment is perhaps the only sin which we are likely to avoid. In all other respects we tend to ape, in cruder forms, the vices of those who are our employers. We lie with our own lips, steal and murder with our own hands, while they, as a rule, do the same things by proxy or under the cover of forms of law. Also we are farther removed from the sweet influences of beauty which must have enriched your life We must continually struggle, and so are always aware of each other's existence We are brothers not in the sense that we feel love, but because we know that we are the children of a common necessity. It is more a question of having felt hunger.

"But what makes our lives wretched is not so much poverty and hunger as the desire to escape from them You, and those like you, gave us this desire You urged us to be ambitious, to make good, to rise in the world, sometimes encouraging the most blatant and outrageous motives of greed and self-indulgence, sometimes pointing us towards the pleasures of the soul— culture, poetry, beauty of manners Did you never observe that if we were to follow your advice we should have to fight and kill our brothers? For there can be no culture and no self-expression without power, and power must always corrupt the soul. When you use such phrases as 'the dignity of man' meaning the dignity of the individual, you are speaking of oppression, for there is nothing dignified about the cruel and crippled existence of the self-seeking man at most he may be an object for compassion "

Here the Professor interrupted, for he was anxious, even in his present situation, that his outlook on life should not be misunderstood "You are using the very words," he said, "that I might use myself I have always agreed with the view that the tyrant himself is no better than a slave"

"It is not possible," said the old man, "to be better than a slave. It is not possible to be higher than the lowest. That is what I am saying, and with that you do not agree At one time I did not believe this myself, although I have had much better opportunities for finding it out than you have had. In my youth I did not see what is now so obvious to me, the unity of the poor, of the slaves, of the powerless with the living world Instead I was disgusted with instances of cruelty and lack of intelligence When I saw husbands and fathers torturing their wives and children I was shocked I despised those who earned their living as spies in factories or as cheats in fairs Looking away from my own people I came to admire those who, like yourself, seemed independent of crime and folly. By learning and study I attempted to raise myself, without ever thinking that in this world no one can raise himself without trampling on another I came to believe that by devotion to truth and beauty a person might shape for himself out of the general mass a noble life, something full and complete Love also entered into my calculations I married, was delighted with my wife's beauty, and justified the pleasures of sensuality by a number of postures which I had learnt from books of romance. My aim was, I think, a classical one to live fully, employing all my energies to enjoy and to inspect my world"

The Professor nodded his head "*Totus*," he said, "*teres atque rotundus*, I beg your pardon"

"I know Latin," said the old man in a low voice. He con-

tinued at once "As you have rightly pointed out, such a view
of life implies the belief that the world is either good or intelli-
gible It was not for some time that I discovered that it was
neither And it may surprise you to know that it was no
economic factor, no sudden realization of injustice, that changed
my mind These things, no doubt, played their part Of course,
I lacked the leisure to read and the money to buy books which
I wanted Hard work in the house, insufficient food, and sleepless nights soon took bloom away from my wife's beauty And
for this I held the economic system responsible I was, what
my son is now, a revolutionary, and I began to feel that I should
be compensated for the disappointments of my own life if I
could prepare the way for a brilliant, logical and scientific
future

"When I was between the ages of thirty and forty I used to
spend several hours a week in teaching Latin, Greek, and
Ancient History to a young boy, the son of one of my friends
This, too, was among my compensations for what I was now
dimly aware was my own failure to live the complete life The
boy appeared both beautiful and strong His mind was infinitely more sensitive and retentive than my own indeed, I
have never met anyone with a keener intelligence or a more
lovable nature And this boy, I was sure, would, with the help
which I was giving him, be able to win scholarships to the
university and become either a world-famous scholar or, better
still, a leader whom even our opponents would have to respect

"Something happened which happens every day, and yet it
took me completely by surprise. One evening this boy surprised me by doing his work less well than usual. Some
important and quite well-known event in ancient history, had
slipped from his memory. I spoke sharply to him and he
appeared puzzled both at my sharpness and his own forgetful-
ness He mentioned that he was not feeling very well, having
fainted while lying on his bed that morning I made inquiries
from the boy's parents and we soon discovered that he had
developed epilepsy None of his brothers and sisters had
suffered from the disease, and there had been no reason whatever to anticipate that he would contract it We did what we
could. It was nearly time for the boy's examinations and so,
while he still visited me, I did not press him for work I knew
that already he was greatly superior to his competitors. Then
I saw what affected me more than anything had affected me

"Often previously I had watched the disintegration of health and physique in the persons of my friends, their wives, and their children For this I blamed the economic system Now I watched the disintegration of a mind For as the boy's fits increased in frequency and violence his memory, and even his capacity for logical thought, began more and more rapidly to deteriorate It was pathetic to see him struggling with sentences which, only a week ago, would have been as clear to him as daylight Well, the boy died, and I was present when he died, brutishly, like a wounded rabbit, showing no glimmer of the beauty and intelligence that had so charmed and delighted all who knew him

"How was I to explain this? This time it was not the economic system that was to blame No medical attention could have saved the boy moreover the same thing was no doubt happening every day in the families of the rich Indeed this one example of cruel death must be multiplied by millions and thousands of millions if my picture of the world was to approach accuracy This was no human crime that could be half-justified by a consideration of human maladjustments This was a divine crime, part of the texture of the Universe, and among the commonest of all events

"I had lost for some time the faith which had been taught to me at achool I did not believe in God, but my belief in my own manhood, in the possibility of the full life, implied a belief that there was nothing in the universe necessarily opposed to human goodness and human reason What ideas of goodness or reason could ever justify the sudden and horrible crippling and destruction of beauty and youth and hope? I began to open my eyes farther, and I saw death, evil, pain, and disease everywhere Now I saw that death is not a human institution, pain was not invented by the governing class, evil and disappointment may be alleviated in some cases by material adjustments, but they spring from the soul of man

"One night, at about this time, I came home late and saw my wife's body lying upon our bed Her hands on the coarse blanket were no longer white and smooth as they had been when I first loved her, but were now rough, chapped, and dirty There was nothing about her that could remind one of a picture of a princess Her face was red and sweating and, since she had a cold, she was snoring through a half-open mouth As I looked at her I realized how rapidly that big body was approach-

ing middle age, debility, and ugliness, and how certainly in the
end it would decay and be eaten by maggots At that moment
I loved her for the first time, for at that moment I loved in her
what was common to all men, what was mortal, corruptible,
full of pain and evil Previously I had loved her for qualities
which had seemed to me outstanding and exceptional, a more
than normal beauty and intelligence I had watched my love
fade away from month to month and from year to year, and
had fancied that the reason for its fading was our poverty
In a well-organised society, I would say, love will be possible,
thus compensating myself for my private disappointment But
now I saw that no social organization can make the body, born
to decay and growing into death, anything but squalid and
pitiable

"I used to go to the seaside on holidays and expect beauty
now I observed more closely the infinite cruelty and indifference
of the sea There is nothing good in rocks or pieces of wood
or feathers The universe which I had imagined as a spectator,
the universe of which goodness and reason Were component
parts, disappeared with a startling rapidity It had never
existed except as a dream into which I had attempted to thrust
myself from out of the world of the living

"Now I began to understand how gravely I had imperilled
my soul In my desire for humanity, for the complete life,
I had almost lost contact with men and women. In my "complete life" there has been nothing but ambition for abstractions,
and I was saved from damnation only because my ambitions
were never realized"

Once more the Professor interrupted. He had listened with
interest and sympathy to the old man's story, although he was
conscious that his own mind, over-wrought by his recent
experiences, was not capable of the concentration that was
required by what was evidently a sincere statement of faith
He observed that the cat was rubbing its head against his legs
Now he asked, "What exactly do you mean by damnation?"

Old Jinkerman spoke in a tired voice His long speech had
evidently exhausted him, and he lay back in his chair, motionless except when his lips moved "I mean," he said, "by damnation a state of mind which I am afraid, my friend, must be your
state   It is the pretended detachment from evil, pain, and
death   It is the denial of Our Saviour's words 'God is Love'

It is the attempt to gloss over the truth that man's life is infinitely wretched "

The Professor inquired humbly "But if God is love, is it not our duty to make the world a better place for men to live in?"

"Do you believe in God?" asked the old man, and the Professor replied: "I cannot say that I do—or not in any orthodox sense of the word But I believe most firmly in the highest ethical ideals of humanity"

The old man leant forward and began to speak with peculiar earnestness "Let me implore you," he said, "before it is too late, to think about your soul and about your brothers and sisters who are alive We do not know what will happen to our souls after death, but we know that, even in life, the soul's eye may become blinded Love has nothing to do with ideals Love is our only hold on life and on truth Love is what we feel for our fellow-men in misery and in terror If the world were what you would have it there would be no love, but the world will always be afflicted, and he who is most afflicted is most lovable With love, death and disease and pain and evil become understandable, for all misery is created as a field in which love may move And when we say 'resist not evil' we do not mean that by setting a good example we shall cause evil to disappear. Death and corruption are strands out of which our life is formed Lust and cruelty are tortures ingrained in the soul How can we resist our world? Our world calls to us, not for resistance, but for love and for pity and for mercy There is nothing to fear in what is so common and inevitable as death and sickness There is only one thing to fear, the damnation of the soul, the incapacity to feel compassion for the infinite suffering of the living, the illusion that something complete may be made of a man's life And that is why I said that neither war nor poverty is so dangerous to mankind as is your liberation For you, in your detachment, endeavour to legislate for the abstract man What a terrible insult to real living and tortured men and women! What a denial of God! What a mutilation of yourself!

"For myself I think with horror of your legislation, your organization, your democracies, aristocracies—your words that are so far away from faces and the inner tremors of the heart Your-isms are so many lashes across the real face of the living Believe me when I say that the world is alive. It lives in suffer-

ing, and that suffering calls not for regulations, not even for
understanding, but for love "

The Professor interrupted "Must not love be active, then?"
he said. "Must not love seek to alleviate some, at least, of the
suffering?"

"I do not think," said the old man, "that you are speaking
of love at all Can love stand above its object? Can love pass
laws? Can love use force? Moreover love is not afraid of the
things which you, even though you have never felt them, still
fear. Pain, poverty, sudden death are not so terrible as you
would have them. But to lose the sense of one's unity with the
living, to lose the power to love, how terrible that is That is
the damnation of the soul That is to lose all beauty and everything divine It is to place oneself beyond the possibility of
redemption

"Suffering is our atmosphere, and death is what we were born
for. Poverty and war, evil in themselves, I grant you, may
often recall a man to a realization of his world But your
philosophy, my friend, can only lead men farther from themselves and farther from God You would abolish poverty in the
name of science, not in the name of love Even now you cannot
see that the poor are richer in their sense of unity in suffering
than are even the most cultivated and æsthetic among the
wealthy. You might abolish poverty if you had your way, but
in so doing you would lose far more than you had gained In
your scientific world evil, under the most specious names,
would come to be an accepted morality. For the aim of your
science would be a brutal and mechanic efficiency, not the salva-
tion of the soul through love Your scientists would eliminate
the weak, not see in them their own faces Love in time might
come to mean merely the attraction between individuals of the
opposite sexes, the short period when a bodily need causes a
momentary and misleading awareness of the existence of another
creature. Oh, my friend, I can see the world that you, no doubt
with the best intentions, would build—a world bright, new,
spick and span, with a brittle confidence, a world free from
economic injustice, but with the whole evil of the soul poising
to break over it like a sea "

The old man stopped abruptly. His face, as he looked across
the room towards the Professor, showed a timidity or diffidence
that presented a strange contrast to the tones of his voice which,
throughout the entire conversation, had been clear and exact.

Now he appeared like a person who fears that he has in some way overstepped the mark, has involuntarily wounded another's feelings, or alluded to some subject that were better left unmentioned

There was something almost pitiable in the old man's expression, and the Professor smiled at him, as if to show that he had taken no offence at what had been said, before himself beginning "Might it not, my dear sir, be just possible—"

Then he heard distinctly the sound of steps in the narrow passage outside the door, and in a moment the whole scene in which he had been playing a part—the cobbler, the scanty carpet, the sleeping cat, and the emphatic words—receded as a dream recedes from his active attention, perhaps to be resuscitated later All his thought was now bent on anxiety for the safety of his son and of Clara and of the young Jinkerman So strong, indeed, was his emotion that, failing in his usual politeness, he left his sentence half-finished and rose to his feet, forgetful of his host, just as the door in that narrow space opened inwards against the arm of the chair in which he had been sitting

CHAPTER XI

THE SURVIVORS

ALREADY in his mind's eye he seemed to see Clara's tall and swaying figure, the perplexed and honest visage of his son; and it was this imagination rather than any vivid impression of the real world or even any exercise of logical analysis that seemed now to set him up once more balanced and self-confident. For now all the old man's talk of pity began to appear to him as some wretched illusion, a morbid mode of thinking, pitiable itself, a brooding over rotten and indistinguishable things, the very pit and seething of life But his own love was like brilliant and independent bronze, shaped out of sorrow, perhaps, impermanent too, capable of tragedy, but none the less definite, ambitious, and divine So he looked towards the door and even his anxiety for his son gave way to his longing to see the Woman in whom he trusted more deeply and could, as he thought, understand more fully than fathers can trust or understand their children

It was with a shock, then, both of surprise and of disappoint-

ment that he saw neither young Jinkerman nor Clara nor his
son, but carefully protruding into the room the large head and
broad shoulders of the representative of the Orthodox Trade
Unions Nor was the unexpectedness of this visit the only
thing which might have caused surprise The whole appearance
of the big man was altered His face was pale, his eyes furtive,
and even the movements of his neck and of his thick fingers
which grasped the edge of the door suggested a failure of nerve,
uncertainty, and apprehension The sight of the professor
seemed to cause in the Trade Unionist a number of involuntary
and unnecessary actions He cleared his throat, stiffened his
neck, placed one hand upon his tie, and for a moment his eyes
assumed that expression of belligerence and of pomposity with
which the Professor had been familiar. And it was in a way
pathetic to observe for how short a time this artificial attitude
could be preserved, for in an instant the show of grandeur and
of independence passed and once more this big man presented
the appearance of a hunted animal, clumsy and uncouth, forced
to defend itself in strange conditions and out of its element

He was evidently as surprised to see the Professor as the
Professor had been to see him, and so for the moment he seemed
to forget the purpose of his visit and the presence of the elder
Jinkerman, who remained sitting in his chair, motionless except
that the beginnings of a smile just curved his lips. The Trade
Unionist opened his mouth wide, as though he were about to
make some statement, emphatic and reassuring as his statements in the past had been; but his pose lacked dignity Only
the upper part of his body was visible from inside the room,
and this trunk was projected horizontally forward so that the
politician presented the appearance rather of a ship's figurehead
or of a jack-the-box than of an authority on any subject In
the past it would have been difficult to have imagined an occasion on which words would fail this man, but now he had no
words at his command, and the Professor would never know
whether the first impulse of his late colleague had been to excuse
to accuse, to commiserate, or to encourage.

Nothing that he could have said, however, could show
wretchedness more clearly than this inability to speak, and the
Professor, with a show of deference, stepped away from the
door, indicating with his hand that the newcomer should climb
over the arm of his chair into the room In stepping backward
he had either kicked or trodden upon the cat which, almost

throughout his long conversation with the old man, had maintained an upright posture on the strip of carpet in front of the
fireplace. This animal, with a shrill squall, now bounded away
from his feet and towards the door, while the Trade Unionist, as
though he were being seriously menaced, at once withdrew his
head and shoulders into the passage way The Professor
secured the cat and, holding it under his arm, patted it as if it
were a dog "There, there!" he said, "I beg your pardon, I am
sure, my dear animal" And it was in this changed atmosphere
that finally the Trade Union official climbed into the room

He addressed his first words to the elder Jinkerman, and as he
spoke there was something timorous in his demeanour which
made him appear to the Professor like a small boy diffidently
excusing himself to a schoolmaster for some negligence in work
or breach of rules In other circumstances the Professor would
have smiled to see this strange metamorphosis of the robust
union man, but now, apart from their danger, he could not help
feeling somehow involved in the other's sense of guilt This
feeling was, no doubt, simply the effect of proximity, for, the
room being so small, he was standing elbow to elbow beside his
late colleague, so close that he could feel against his arm the
very pressure of the other's heavy breathing As he looked at
the calm face of Jinkerman, who had not stirred from his chair,
he began to feel that he too was being arraigned, and for a
moment thought of the cat, which he still held underneath his
arm, as of some object, perhaps incriminating and at least
undignified, of which he must rid himself at once He put one
foot in the fireplace, withdrawing himself a little from the big
man at his side, set the cat on the narrow mantelpiece, and now
surveyed in a more objective spirit the scene before him

It was a timid voice that the Trade Unionist began "I don't
know whether you remember me, sir"

Jinkerman interrupted, "I remember you very well, though
I think it must be twenty years since we last spoke together"

"You knew my father," said the Trade Unionist, and in his
voice was a note of supplication "I have come to ask for
shelter"

"Your father," said the old man, "was my colleague at a time
when I, like you, was foolish enough to busy myself with politics
And, if my memory is not at fault, when I last spoke with you
I endeavoured to persuade you not to waste some of the best
years of your life as both your father and I had done I pointed

out how in politics even a man who sets out delibeiately to serve others will in the end be betrayed into the pursuit of personal ambition I showed you how you would spend your life in unworthy intrigues, and how your greatest effects on the masses would be secured by pomposity, affectation, and insincerity I pointed out that to be successful you would have to imitate not the few virtues but the innumerable hypocrisies of our oppressors Above all you would lose the power of loving I can see that you have done so, but I cannot condemn you Perhaps now, if you would realize to the full your own wretchedness, you might save your soul"

"They have destroyed our printing press," said the Trade Unionist gravely The Professor noticed that large tears had appeared in the corners of his eyes, giving him the appearance of some stupid but amiable stag

He broke in upon the conversation "But, my dear fellow," he said, "what can they have against you? Why, they actually made use of your name in order to discredit me"

The Trade Unionist's voice was feeble "I know," he said "I have always been against—" He stumbled in his speech, then continued "I have always occupied—" But now his well-worn formulas seemed to fail him He was wholly at a loss for words and the tears swelled up bigger and bigger in his simple outraged eyes After a long pause he again opened his mouth and said, "They have killed Uncle Henry "

The Professor was about to speak when his eyes fell upon the elder Jinkerman The old man had relaxed his body in the chair; his eyes were closed and his hands clasped below his chin as though in prayer In silence they listened to his whispered words "O Love," he was saying, "throw your blanket over this torturing day Over pain, violation, and death let your sweet profusion pour To those whose hopes are shattered reveal, Love, the barrenness of all hope Let those who are dying be sure of how common a thing death is Let those who are betrayed pity their betrayers. Show us, Love, how general and inevitable is our misery, how every action is a hot breeding place for sin and death. But you alone, Love, are pure and holy Among festering sores, in disease and corruption you alone remain sane and wholesome And over the more terrible and piercing ills of the spirit, perverse cruelty, desperate lust, indoctrinated hate, you, Love, still, like an owl, stretch your soft and silent wings Teach us, Love, not to shrink back in horror from the full beastliness of man. His body made to rot and stink, his soul, tortured by unrecognized fears, mistaken ambitions, envies, and delusive lusts, help us none the less, Love, to see him as the most abject thing in nature, and most abject, most truly pitiable, when most proud Let the sufferers to-day exult in the communion of their sufferings, in the startling revelation of their instability But have mercy, Love, upon the lonely and self-centred oppressors Lead them, Love, into thy peace! Lead them "

The Professor interrupted the prayer in a voice that was, for him, unusually high and sharp "No! No!" he cried, and then his eyes fell upon the Trade Union leader who was standing, with his eyes closed and hands clasped together, attending in the most docile manner to the words of one whom now he seemed prepared again to acknowledge as a preceptor At the interruption the Trade Unionist opened one eye, and as the Professor proceeded he opened another, but he seemed to attach little importance to what was being said

"You may keep your purity," said the Professor "But, for my part, I would throw it all away if by so doing I could save a little of that life and that confidence which you so greatly despise Oh, how can you be pitiful and not indignant? The bodies are beautiful, if only for a time"

He paused, searching for words with which to embody the shame and loathing which he had felt while listening to what appeared to him as the old man's capitulation before the forces of chaos He saw in his imagination the liquid eyes and living flesh of Clara and was resolved, whatever might be the future of either the soul or the body, to protect, so far as he could, what he knew to be lovely from violation. Yet before he found the words for which he sought he remembered the scene which had taken place only the day before, though now it seemed long ago, during his lectures on Sophocles He remembered his son's interruption and his own plea for a rational examination of all impulses that originated in the emotions He smiled and began, as though it were some machine, to set his mind to work, seeking farther back in the old man's argument for some logical fallacy or some incorrect statement of fact But hardly had he become conscious of this shifting in his own attention when once more his thoughts were interrupted by a swelling roar of sound

Intermittently during the last hours he had been aware of

the noise of engines in the air. Now, with a startling suddenness, the air became filled and overflowed with the sound It
was as though a squadron of planes were about to alight on the
roof of the house Previously the narrow congested room in
which he, the Trade Unionist, and the cat were so tightly packed
together and in which old Jinkerman with his prophetic utterances had alone seemed at ease, had appeared to him as being
the scene, not quite of a nightmare, but certainly of a dream,
so abrupt had been his transition from the broken hopes which
he had entertained at the Chancellory, from his ignominious
hurry through the streets to this mean and unfamiliar closet
While he had listened to the old man's strange and confident
expression of faith, even while the had observed the changed
demeanour of the Trade Unionist, he had regarded himself
rather as an involuntary spectator than as an actor of the scene
This room to him had been a temporary and a somewhat unreal
retreat from the more spacious world in which he was certainly
a fugitive but which he imagined that he understood But now
the outer world seemed to have become all one metallic roar
and drone

The small window rattled in the dreadful vibration. The
Trade Unionist, stumbling over the Professor's foot, plunged
on to the floor and buried his face in the seat of the unoccupied
chair Old Jinkerman had raised his eyebrows in surprise, but
he did not turn his head

The Professor stepped carefully over the calves of the Trade
Unionist, pronouncing the words "Excuse me," and then
hoisted himself up from the arm of the old man's chair so that
he could see out of the window First he looked cautiously
downwards and saw that the window did not open upon the
street, but only upon sloping red roofs and chimney pots.
Jerking down the sliding frame he put out his head and saw
that all the sky that he could see was filled with the black
triangular wings and long bodies of bombing planes With some
difficulty he twisted round his neck and looked back into the
room. "Planes," he said, "no doubt from beyond the frontier,"
but the noise was now so enormous that no one, even had
anyone been listening, could have heard his voice He turned
again from the room and contemplated, as though it were a
pageant, the low-flying giant, shapes that were the first demonstration of his country's loss of independence

The sky was blue and cloudless, but the sky itself, where

silence could be imagined, seemed cut away, removed to another dimension by the black lines of roaring bombers These bird shapes oppressed the city, and the continuous noise of their machinery was like that of a drill grinding on the ear and on the nerves beyond the ear. So close and menacing did the planes appear that for a moment the Professor expected death, whether in the form of high explosive or of gàs, to be rained down from their big bodies He was soon, however, aware that he was the witness of a mere parade. From some of the planes showers of white leaflets were falling to the ground, and one of these leaflets, having been swept upwards or downwards by some eddy in the air, was blown on to the roof below the window through which he peered Straining his eyes he was able to make out the word FREEDOM, printed in heavy black type and forming part of one of the headlines, but that was the only word which he could decipher, and soon another current of air swept the small and flapping paper down the slope of the roof and into the street below

More and more planes flowed across the sky, and the drilling roar of their engines was now a persistent atmosphere, but the Professor did not comment in his mind upon the increasing sound, nor speculate on the numbers of machines which were passing before his eyes He thought only that this mass of metal, this interminable din was tyrannizing over flesh and blood Reason could hardly exist now where words had to be shouted Resistance was futile with the whole sky, and soon the ground, already occupied by the enemy. He saw in his mind's eye the masses of his fellow citizens whom that morning he had planned to address and to reassure people who, for the most part, had no very pronounced views on politics, but whom he had wished to rally as a unanimous force behind certain obvious and great ideas He would have appealed to them as free men to support what they understood as freedom: but now the word, in lying headlines, had been dropped from implements of oppression and was swept along the gutters of the streets The various faces that earlier in the day he could have imagined intent as they listened to his words would now be blank with bewilderment, or terrified, or hysterical These black and swinging shapes of steel had broken the discipline of the day, broken it, he saw already, beyond repair. There would be no more confident acquiescence in regular habits, let alone any innovation, but now only uncertainty, loss of will, the

scramble for individual advantage What he was seeing was the
violation of a whole people, the tearing of a civilization out of
the fabric of history Yet as his mind was appalled by the
contrast between this weight of flying metal and the soft faces
and limbs, generally lovable, the more or less rational natures
of his fellow citizens, he began to reflect that these machines
also had been made and were controlled by human hands
Were the hands that dug the metal and shaped it, were the
brains, he wondered, that had calculated stresses, that had
co-ordinated time and space, the hands and the brains of slaves?
Or was it true (for he remembered Vander's words) that there
were large bodies of men living at this time who consciously
aimed, whether from disgust or from mere folly, at wiping off
the face of the earth those ideals which, in his view, had from
the days of Marathon dignified the world of men? He began
to see the throbbing planes as though they were the fierce spots
of some immense disease, studding the sky and infecting the
earth with fever

He felt the pressure of a finger against his back, and turned
to see with a shock of surprise and of anticipation the face of
the young Jinkerman, and behind him, at the door and struggling
to enter the room, the figure of his own son The noise in the
sky had been so great that he had not heard them come in, and
even now, though he could see that Jinkerman was speaking,
he could not hear, so dulled were his ears, what was being said.
For half a second he again had the sensation that he was an
actor in a nightmare, that the whole circumference of his world
might at any moment crack and that all which he saw would be
· dispelled as phantoms in the air. And this feeling, no doubt,
was simply the effect of the overwhelming noise in which men
speaking presented the appearance merely of the dumb figures
of a silent film He did not immediately notice that Jinkerman
was now not dressed as a policeman, and that his lean face was
further disguised by the imposition of an untidy moustache

The Trade Union leader was still kneeling on the floor, an
indistinguishable bulk, with his head buried in the seat of a
chair, and in this posture he reminded the Professor of one of
his uncles whom he could remember as habitually adopting a
similar position at the family prayers which used, in the Professor's childhood, to be held by his father either before or after
breakfast. Young Jinkerman was now standing with his feet
astride the Trade Unionist's legs, and the Professor's son, as

though he were some character in a farce, was insinuating himself through the narrow crack of the door and over the arm of the chair In his efforts to reach the carpet he kicked the prostrate cabinet minister in the ribs, but the big man made no move, as though he were endeavouring, by immobility or protective coloration, to escape the notice of some real or imagined enemy

All this the Professor saw in a flash, but at the same time as he was seeing it he was aware that his heart had begun to beat more rapidly and his eyes to stiffen their attention as he stared at the door to see whether anyone else had been waiting outside for entry. His son had now reached an upright position on the carpet and was standing pressed between the younger Jinkerman and the wall His eyes were much brighter than they had been when he had visited his father that morning. The events of the day seemed to have aged him, to have put resolution and a kind of pitilessness into the expression of his face He stretched out his hand and the Professor, inclining forward from his perch on the window-sill, took it smiling, but even while he was pressing his son's hand he could not keep his eyes away from the narrow and empty crack between the door and the wall He looked inquiringly at Jinkerman, and Jinkerman shook his head, at the same time saying something which was inaudible and motioning to the Professor to close the window

With some difficulty the Professor forced the frame upwards, thus shutting out some at least of the sound which all this time had by no means abated, but had rather increased in volume There was no room for him on the floor, unless he were to stand face to face, as close as though dancing, with one or other of the present occupants of the small area, and so he remained with one foot on the arm of old Jinkerman's chair and the other on the window-sill, raised above the others as if he were an orator or some important figure in a tableau on the stage

Jinkerman shouted at him "I am sorry that I could not get in touch with your friend," and the Professor nodded his head gravely, although when he had heard the words he had felt a sudden constriction at his heart. At the sound of the voice the Trade Unionist raised his head from the chair, but when he saw the room full of people he quickly resumed his first position The Professor's son had recognized him, however, and with an expression of distaste on his face he pointed him out to young Jinkerman, who, pressing his lips together, looked with equal distaste at the back view of the recumbent reformist Old Jinkerman sat up in his chair and made some remark which no one could hear, and then the Professor, as though from the prow of a ship, shouted into the room: "Have you any news ?"

Young Jinkerman edged nearer to the window. He stood on tiptoe while the Professor leant forwards so that his ear was close to the young man's lips "You want to hear about the girl?" Jinkerman said, and as the Professor nodded he began to tell him how he had reached Clara's apartment, but had not dared to enter it as he had seen two men, one of whom was known to him, both wearing the uniform of the Legionaries, go into the room as he was mounting the stairs "Are you sure that she is reliable?" he asked, and the Professor, with a smile that showed both sadness and affection, again nodded his head As Jinkerman did not proceed he added "She is perhaps trying on her own account to do what she can for my safety Perhaps ." But Jinkerman interrupted, shouting unnecessarily loud the words, "There is no hope whatever of that" He went on to tell how he had waited for some time, and had not gone away until he had seen two more Legionaries enter the house He would have continued to wait, on the chance of being able to secure an interview later, had it not been for the fact that his plans for an escape had already been worked out and that success depended on their being able to reach the outskirts of the city before the arrival of foreign troops As it was, he said, he had been delayed in his return to the house and now they must start within five minutes He could be reasonably sure, through the aid of comrades who, being less well known than himself, would remain behind, of getting a message through to Clara within the next two or three days

The Professor's arms were now aching with the effort that had been required to sustain him in his position on the window, sill He lowered himself on to the floor, and now he, his son, and the younger Jinkerman were standing close together, their faces only inches apart and their arms around each other's shoulders, piesentmg the appearance of a group of statuary or of the somewhat disorganized front row of a scrum Old Jinkerman was sitting still behind his son's back, and the Professor, by peeping between the necks of the two standing figures, could see the broad bottom of the Trade Union leader, who remained kneeling on the hearth-rug, though whether or not he had raised his head it was impossible to say.

The Professor looked into Jinkerman's eyes. "First of all," he said, "I should like to thank you for what you have done," but the other had not been able to hear his words, so the Professor repeated them, raising his voice Jinkerman made no reply. He waited for the Professor to continue, and the Professor noticed from this close view that he had a small mole below his ear He counted the hairs on this mole and found that there were five Then he said "I am afraid that I shall not be able to Come with you "

There was a disturbance in the closely-packed group The Professor's son had taken his hand from behind Jinkerman's neck and was endeavouring to thrust it in the direction of his father The effect of this action had been to make Jinkerman take a step backward, and in doing so he had trodden upon the cat, which squalled loudly and, leaping on to the chair above the Trade Unionist's head, arched its back and emitted an ear-splitting shriek This noise, together with the continuous reverberation of sound from outside, seemed so unearthly that for a moment they all stood silent, gazing at the cat as though it were some prodigy, and the Professor's son let his hand he lightly pressed upon his father's stomach The cat slid down behind the chair and the Professor, looking at his son, observed that the young man's expression had softened and that he was pleading with him to change his mind Wriggling his shoulders he took the hand from his waistcoat and pressed it

"Good luck to you," he said "I can only hope that your efforts will be more successful than mine have been" There was a pause during which the Professor thought that he observed tears in his son's eyes "I believe that we stand for the same things," he shouted hurriedly, and relinquished his grip on the young man's hand

Jinkerman inclined his head forward "You would be of great value to us," he said, but the Professor looked at him somewhat sadly, raising his eyebrows, and gently shaking his head He was aware that any opposition that could now be organized against the new tyranny would have to come from those very revolutionary bodies whose existence he had in the past deplored He fancied that, as far as leadership was concerned, his part was played and was only anxious now to save his friends and perhaps his honour

"I am sorry," he said again "I wish you good fortune My mind is made up" Then he inserted an arm between the two

bodies and pointed in the direction of the piostrate figure on
the mat "Why do you not take with you Mr Tubb?" he said

The other two, jostling each other, faced about, and from
behind them the Professor could see that the Trade Unionist
had now raised his head from the shelter of the chair and was
surveying the two revolutionaries, whose party he had in the
past so frequently and vehemently attacked, with frightened
imploring eyes The Professor, leaning forward, could just hear
his son's voice, vibrant with a kind of bitterness that was strange
to him, "What good is he to us?" But whether he had been
affected by the thought of the uselessness of recriminations or
whether the sight of the big man's pitiable collapse had stirred
his compassion, his voice changed, and he added "There's a
warrant out for him, even if he is a traitor Perhaps he would
be useful"

The Trade Unionist made no reply and at this time appeared,
in the Professor's view, for the first time dignified "Yes," said
Jinkerman suddenly "Remember that things have changed
From now on their enemies must be our friends Of course
we will take him"

The Trade Unionist, with surprising agility, scrambled to his
feet and in so doing forced the others backward against the
wall He then sat down in the chair The lines of his face had
hardened, and now, without taking any further notice of the
others, he leant forward and tapped the elder Jinkerman on the
knee "You were wrong," he shouted "It is necessary to
fight"

The old man did not move He lay back with his hands
extended along the arms of the chair and his eyes closed His
mouth was open and they guessed from the position of his
tongue that he was dead.

The Professor quickly opened the window, releasing into the
room another storm of angry sound Jinkerman knelt down
beside his father and, opening his shirt, placed his ear against
the lifeless flesh "I fear the sudden noise has been too much
for him," said the Professor in a mechanical and horror-struck
undertone He was surprised to hear himself speaking and
relieved that no one had heard his words

Jinkerman rose from the floor and the Professoi noticed that
his eyes were dulled, though his tightly pressed lips afforded no
hint of what his feelings were "We must be going," he said,
and began to push the Trade Unionist towards the door The

Professor's son was next to go, but before he went he turned to his father and again clasped his hand. In the boy's eyes the Professor read such evident affection that for the moment he forgot his real situation and smiled as he might have done had he been congratulating his son on the winning of a race or the passing of an examination Meanwhile the Trade Unionist had turned at the door and was waving to him as though he were setting out on some picnic or boating excursion The Professor waved too, and then gave his attention to Jinkerman who was scribbling an address on a piece of paper

"You may go there," he said, "for to-night, and in any case I shall get a message to you within a day or two And if you want to visit the girl be sure that you wear a disguise You will find material in the next room" The young man paused and turned to look for the last time at the dead body of his father Then he shook the Professor's hand. "Good-bye, sir," he said "You did your best" And then he, too, went quickly from the narrow room

CHAPTER XII

THE CONQUERED

IT was some two hours later that the Professor also made his way into the street After the others had gone he had sat for some time in the empty chair, resting and considering what his course of action should be, but something in the appearance of the dead body which sat facing him had inhibited his thought His eyes had been unable to leave off contemplating the gaunt face, much less noble than in life, of the old cobbler who had so warmly recommended an indiscriminate love Now no tenderness whatever was expressed by the sunken features and the hard lines of eye sockets, chin, and cheek bones over which the skin was drawn so tightly. Nothing but a distorted shape seemed to represent humanity, and the Professor, as he gazed with a feeling of some horror at the collapsed frame, could not help wondering what connection the soul, over whose damnation the old man had been so exercised, could ever have had, or could have now with that graceless flesh. That he, too, would one day, and perhaps very shortly, present an equally wretched spectacle he knew well; and for a moment his mind was overwhelmed by the thought of how numerous were the dead and how few and unsettled the living It was an obvious enough reflection, but at the time it terrified him Numbers, certainly, were on the old man's side. Homer also, and Sophocles, had been dead for ages

He pitied, but he could not love that inhuman face For himself he began to fear death as he had never feared it before, nor could he by any means take as a model for himself the old man's indifference to the common lot Now all the living appeared to him as infinitely pathetic, infinitely lovable, not because of their general suffering and their inevitable end, but because of the hopes which were often realized in life and because of the beauty and goodness which, however transitory, did, he knew, mark almost every life at one time or at another. That for the body death and corruption, for the soul the pangs of cruelty and injustice, seemed by the very structure of the universe to be ordained he did not dispute, but now, facing the dead cobbler, more than ever he was convinced that mere sympathy and commiseration were not enough. To give freedom even for some moments and in a few places to the brief and fantastically daring hopes of the living, their simple and extravagant demands on life and nature—this seemed to him now the only worthy aim of reason He thought of the Trade Unionist's words "You were wrong It is necessary to fight", and he thought of what his son had said on the previous day "I hate because I love" In the past such phrases would have appeared to him as almost meaningless, but now, as he listened to the roar of aeroplanes that still terrified his city, he seemed to see in all forms of tyranny and of subjugation something like that physical death which was before his eyes And if love, he saw clearly now, were to exercise itself in action, love itself would have to be armed

He rose hurriedly from the chair and went into the next room. Here he found some bread and cheese which old Jinkerman had, no doubt, set out for himself earlier in the day The Professor ate what was on the table and, while he was eating, composed, so great was still his sense of civic duty, a letter to the Chief Officer of Health informing him that there was at the address which he gave a dead body to be removed without delay. He smiled wryly as he signed the letter with his own name, for he was reflecting that this was the first letter he had written since he had accepted the post of Chancellor Next he examined the cupboards of the room and found, as he had expected, a great variety of clothes which had been used no doubt from time to time as disguises by the young policeman There were also beards, wigs, and whiskers, but these the Professor rejected He shaved off his moustache and clothed himself in thick boots, corduroy trousers, and old green coat, and a cap which could be pulled down low over his forehead In this costume he imagined that he would be safe enough from detection and, having carefully transferred to his pockets some of his own possessions, including his pocket diary and his gold watch, he went to the street door, opened it cautiously, and stepped into the street.

He noticed first that the noise of the aeroplanes had diminished and, though there were still many of them in the sky, he could see that various groups of these were now flying away from the city, no doubt to the aerodromes which had formed part of the country's system of defence All this time his sense of hearing had been adapting itself to the continuous roar and now the silence made him uneasy, for it seemed to him like some dreadful interval before the denouement of a tragedy or the discovery of a crime There was not even so much as the sound of a footfall in the street, for in this quarter of the town the windows of the houses had their shutters up and the inhabitants remained indoors

So for some time he walked slowly through empty streets and alleys until he came to the road where not long ago he and Jinkerman had been seen and pursued by the vendor of ice creams Even before he reached this road he could hear the noise of shouting, and, on coming out of the side street, he narrowly escaped being run over by a lorry filled with laughing and cheering youths which was being recklessly driven over the pavement Some twenty young men, cheering and singing, filled the lorry itself, and others were sitting astride the bonnet, were clinging to the mudguards, or had perched upon the roof above the driver's head. Some were drinking out of bottles, others throwing bottles into the roadway, and others waving flags They were shouting out comments, either facetious or insulting, on the passers-by, and occasionally such slogans as "United we stand," "Death to the internationalists," and "The Captain has arrived." As the car, with a shrieking of brakes, pulled up on the pavement just short of the Professor, one of the youths tossed him down a small stick to which was attached a flag bearing the Legion colours "Here! Wave that, you blasted proletarian!" one of the young men said, and the Professor dutifully flapped the piece of material up and down, while the driver of the lorry, to a chorus of curses and shouts, managed to back his vehicle into the road. "Hooray for our deliverers!" shouted the young men, and with flushed enthusiastic faces and waving arms they sped on up the street

The Professor retained the flag since he imagined that it would form a useful addition to his disguise There were now no aeroplanes to be seen in the sky and, though in this road there were large crowds of shouting men and women, the sudden silence of the air made all their vociferation seem puny, so that even though he was surrounded by feverish faces, fast-moving vehicles, and demonstrations with banners the Professor could not avoid the feeling that in fact he was among a people who were only half animate

He continued to walk along the pavement in the direction of the Chancellory, but soon had to stop because of a small but compact body of people who had gathered around some object of interest and completely blocked his passage. He succeeded in elbowing his way along the inside of this group, until he could see in the centre a small man on his hands and knees on the pavement and, standing over him, two young men, students whom he could remember as having attended his lectures, both dressed in the uniform of Legionaries Something in the prostrate man's appearance seemed familiar and, looking more closely, he was able to recognize him as Dr Cornelius Chough, the incoherent chairman of the Pacifist meeting which on the previous day he had attended in the park Someone in the crowd had demanded of what crime this elderly explorer was guilty and Dr Chough had raised his head with a grateful, but puzzled, expression on his face

One of the young Legionaries, a tall impressive figure in his neat uniform, turned at once to the crowd and said in a voice of great sincerity, "He is a pacifist-internationalist provocateur."

The other young man, who with his flushed and grinning face appeared a coarser type of person, looked down savagely at his victim "Do you deny that?" he shouted, and at the same time kicked Dr. Chough in the iibs. The old man opened his mouth but, before he had had time to utter anything more than the trumpeting noise which he habitually made before speaking, the young Legionary's boot caught him in the teeth.

While he was spitting blood from his mouth his other perse-
cutor, whose sensitive face was set in a mask of cool righteousness, thrust a piece of chalk into his hands

"Write the following words," he began "'Down with
Internationalist Pacifism.'"

Dr Chough was moving his hands, on which he supported
his trunk, now to the right, now to the left He appeared like
some wounded rat, surrounded by a circle of stocks, and
searching for an outlet in the ring of his enemies There was
no outlet, and so, biting his lip and with blood still oozing from
the corner of his mouth, the old man took up the chalk The
Professor looked in the faces of the spectators. The faces were
cold, pale, and indifferent, so that it would have been impossible
to know whether they viewed this exhibition with approval or
with disgust

Cautiously the Professor sidled past the crowd and went on
his way ; but before he reached the vicinity of the Chancellory
he was stopped by several other such groups, for the chalking
of slogans upon the pavement seemed to have appealed to the
imagination or to the sense of justice of the Legionaries, and so
at intervals of every ten or twenty yards some person, male or
female, was to be found, suspected of democratic sympathies,
of intellectual pretensions, or merely of foreign birth, compelled
by violence and often with brutality to scrawl statements or
exhortations on the stone The streets were full of policemen
and auxiliary policemen, and yet none of these officers made
anywhere the slightest effort to interfere with what was taking
place Everywhere the Professor observed the same apathetic
and indeterminate expressions among the majority of the
spectators and he reflected that no doubt they, as well as he,
were deterred by fear from showing their true feelings And
yet if it had been suggested to him that such things could happen
so quickly and so suddenly, with such an air of righteousness,
in the heart of a city which he had considered civilized, he would
never have accepted the suggestion as probable In spite of his
indignation he now felt, what must be felt in the presence of the
unexpected and ummagmed, a growing terror, and consciously
he pressed his lips tightly together as he walked

He had intended to skirt the Chancellory buildings, but when
he reached the street in which they were situated he observed
that a large crowd had gathered outside, and approaching nearer
he saw that the door and the ground-floor windows had been

broken in, and that the entrance was now protected by a force
of soldiers with fixed bayonets On the steps, where he had
stood yesterday to acknowledge the congratulations of his
fellow citizens, an orator was now standing and haranguing the
crowd By his side a sham gallows had been erected, and from
this depended an effigy which the Professor did not immediately
recognize as having been designed to represent himself Confident in his disguise, he joined the crowd and gave his attention
to the orator, a thick-set man with a red face who from time to
time as he was speaking wiped away with a large yellow handkerchief the drops of sweat from his forehead and from his neck
above the collar of his uniform

"As for the Professor," he was saying, "if only he'd stuck to
his rotten foreign poetry, we would have nothing against him
You might think that because he spent his time on such trash
he was harmless That would be a great mistake He used his
reputation for scholarship in order to make all kinds of international contacts, most of them being, naturally, of a subversive
nature Oh yes, I know that in his speeches he used to refer to
national unity But what did he mean by it? For him the phrase
was a rotten intellectualist catchword Of the unity of race, of
the fellow-feeling of blood, of the joyous subordination of
comrades to their real and mystical chief, this wretched pedant
had no conception His low and grovelling mind could rise no
higher than the barren details of economics, wages and hours.
And this is the man who is supposed to be an authority on
poetry! I tell you that he has no poetic fire, no mysticism, no
capacity for either love or hate. He called himself a democrat,
a dingy enough term, but in reality he was far worse His real
views were demomo-absolutistic. His mean and envious nature
made him a fomenter of class-war He was like a mole working
in the dark, continually with his sophistries undermining the
loyalty of the nation and the sanctity of the home."

At this point the speech was interrupted by the emergence from
the crowd in front of the steps of a gaunt and elderly woman,
wearing a large black straw hat and carrying an umbrella The
speaker appeared at first indignant at her appearance but, after
she had given the Legionary salute, he allowed her to mount
the steps until she stood just below the comic effigy of the
Professor that dangled from the mock gallows The old woman
turned to the crowd and in a precise voice announced "I am
the Resurrection and the Life" She then faced about and,

holding her umbrella by the middle, struck the effigy three brisk blows in the face After this she went quietly down the steps and rejoined the crowd

The speaker, on her disappearance, rubbed his hands together as if he were a showman, and prepared once more to address the gathering: but the old woman's action had stirred other members of his audience to express their feelings more overtly. A young and pretty girl, bare-headed and with unusually large eyes, darted forward to the steps and spat at the cloth face below the gallows "Down with nasty free love!" she shouted "We don't want any of it here" Then she returned to the protection of the arm of a large, red-faced, and rather stupid-looking boy, her brother perhaps, or her fiancé Others also began to move towards the steps and to attack the effigy with umbrellas, walking sticks, or with their bare hands. The speaker raised his voice in an attempt to restore order, but the weight and movement of the crowd were too much for him, and soon he had to retire past the fixed bayonets of the sentries into the shelter of the Chancellory

The Professor watched while one person seized an arm, another a leg, another the head of the foolish image of himself, and while in small groups, running and shouting, they carried off their trophies into the streets The crowd, he noticed, seemed to be composed chiefly of shopkeepers, bank-clerks, and their wives, though there were also present some who from their dress might belong to wealthier classes By what action of his life, he wondered, could he have aroused the hostility of these people? He remembered some of the words of Vander, which now seemed to him like a prophecy It was true, it seemed, that beneath the apparent surface calm of Christian and democratic civilization wild and unsatisfied forces were waiting for a day of destruction, and now the day was at hand He began to see how miserable and thwarted must have been the lives of these people who now so feverishly and abjectly hurried for an excuse for passion and an image of enthusiasm, and he pitied, while he feared, the reeling bodies and the distorted faces

He now began to make his way towards the park, for Clara's apartment was situated at its farther side beyond the University The park was less crowded than he had expected to find it Bands were playing on the grass, but very few people were listening to them. The Professor noticed the stand still placarded with advertisements for Miss de Lune's nudist organization, but now no nudist was to be seen What people there were on the paths were heading in a direction opposite to that on which he was going, and he received a severe shock when one of the passers-by stopped him and looked inquiringly into his face The professor recognized at once the well-dressed proprietor of the shop for gas-masks which he had visited while on his way to take up the position of Chancellor, and for the moment he forgot his disguise while his mind hesitated between the alternative of pleading with the shopkeeper not to betray his identity or of taking to his heels But the next instant he saw that he had not been recognized

The shopkeeper addressed him calmly, "My man," he said, "you should be going in the opposite direction" He had spoken as he might have spoken to an object of considerably less importance than a dog or cat, and so unused was the Professor still to his altered circumstances that his first impulse was to express his distaste at the other's rudeness. He said nothing, and the shopkeeper continued, "We want everyone on the streets to welcome the troops Our deliverers, you know"

"I am on urgent business," said the Professor, attempting rather unsuccessfully to disguise his voice His clothes, however, were disguise enough "Then don't stand here wasting your time," the shopkeeper replied "Hurry, my man, hurry!" He caught sight of the flag which the Professor was still holding somewhat shamefacedly behind his back. "Stop a moment!" he said, and took slowly from his pocket a handful of coins from which, after some deliberation, he selected a small piece of silver. "Here you are, my man," he said, as he pressed the com into the Professor's hand "Don't spend it all on drink It's a great day." And without taking further notice of him he began to walk away slowly down the path The Professor watched him go, and was particularly irritated by his long swinging strides and by the sight of his top hat Then he turned round and, avoidmg the main pathways, cut across the Park towards' the University buildings

It was possible for him to reach the back of the University without passing through the streets of expensive shops through which he had gone on the morning of the previous day ; indeed, he might have avoided the University altogether, but fancying himself safe in his disguise he could not forbear from going by the route he knew well and from revisiting, if only for a short passage, the walls within which he had spent the greater part of his life and which, as was evident, he would have now for an indefinite period to leave And as he approached the grey and crumbling stone with which the University was surrounded, he began to wonder whether or not he would have done better if he had never left or never entered these precincts The memory of the exasperated crowd tearing avidly to pieces an object of cloth and wool was still fresh in his mind, and at the same time he thought of the many hours which he had spent on the recension of the text of Sophocles, on his translation of the Oresteia and on his research into the antiquities of the Hittite Empire Such specialized work would have even now, he supposed, a certain value, but in those areas of life in which he had attempted to exercise his full personality all his efforts had been frustrated. A new thought struck him What use would the present government have for Homer? What use for any form of exact scholarship? The Professor began to wish that there were more people in the country who possessed a knowledge of Greek

He had now reached the walls of the University buildings, and turning out of the park came to an open space of ground from which he could see the window of his own bedroom Below the window a number of students were gathered together about a structure of some kind which seemed to be causing them considerable amusement The Professor pulled his cap down over his forehead and approached nearer Looking upward he observed with a shock so sharp that it seemed like pain that one of the students was in his bedroom and was from time to time tossing down his books to the crowd below He now saw that what was occupying the attention of the crowd was a pile of volumes, all, he fancied, taken from his own shelves, and that near the pile had been placed two cans of petrol On a chair, elevated above the rest, stood the student whom he remembered as having replied to his son's interruption during his lecture This young man was dressed in Legionary uniform but had put a mortar-board on his head and was engaged in making a speech which, from the burst of laughter and excited plaudits of his audience, seemed to be of a humorous nature Soon the Professor became aware that what he was witnessing was intended to be an impersonation of himself

"My dear young friends," the student was saying, and he took off an imaginary pair of glasses and wiped them—a gesture which aroused a roar of approbation from the crowd "My dear young friends, will you perhaps allow me to suggest to your minds one or two ideas with reference to the Polls?"

"Police! Police! Catch him, boys!" interjected a spectator from the back of the audience, a sally that was greeted with a fresh burst of laughter

The main speaker continued "The Polis, my dear friends, is a very important word beginning with a P"

"Damn the bloody Polis!" shouted another interrupter. "Let's get on with the job"

"Certainly, certainly, my friends," said the speaker "I must of course, accept a majority decision, such being the undoubted practice of all democrats Let us then, by all means, get on with the job And first of all let me say that we are assembled here together to do justice on a number of what certain people have described as bloody lousy old books Personally I should hesitate, before making use of such an expression myself, and indeed I am inclined to think that there is much to be said on both sides of this question We shall therefore, in condemning or absolving these volumes, abide strictly, like the bloody fine democrats we are, to the will of the majority Now, let's see what we have here" He reached down from his chair and picked up two finely-bound volumes which the Professor immediately recognized as his interleaved and annotated edition of Homer

"Now, here," said the speaker, "we have two books, one of which is called *Iliad* and the other *Odyssey* The author, I'm afraid, must be so obscure or so ashamed of himself that his name does not appear on the outside, and I'm damned well not going to bother to look inside Now has anyone got a good word to say for these books?"

A tall, nervous-looking youth said, "I believe, Mr. Chairman, that they are about war" He then appeared still more ill at ease, as though he regretted having drawn attention to himself, but his face brightened when the speaker replied "A very good point, sir A very good point" His face immediately fell, however, as the speaker continued "I must say, nevertheless, that it seems to me a pretty bad show that any Legionary should have spent his time reading these books" The tall young man blushed, and muttered, "I haven't read them all," but no one could hear his remark and, having looked once or twice sheepishly from side to side as though to observe how he was regarded by his companions, he subsided into silence.

The speaker was still holding the books at arm's length "These books," he said, "are not only in a foreign language, but are not even printed intelligibly Is our national alphabet good enough for us, or is it not?" A roar of applause greeted this rhetorical question, and the young man at once threw the books to the ground "A little petrol, please, James," he said "This handsomely bound trash will make a good beginning"

The Professor had impulsively started to move forward, but almost at once he realized the true facts of his situation He watched the flames biting into the yellow calf of the two books and it seemed to him as though years of his life were being cauterized He stood on the outskirts of the crowd with one or two other spectators who were obviously not of the University, but even here he knew that he was not wholly safe from detection Still he could not take his eyes away from the scene before him and, if the bitterness of his feelings had not been so great, his eyes would perhaps have filled with tears as he noticed among the crowd many students, in addition to the young speaker, who had attended his lectures, and some whom he had regarded as promising pupils

The speaker was now holding up another book "Here," he said, "we have an edition of the poems of a chap called Keats Can anyone show any just impediment why this book should not join the bonfire? I believe, by the way, that the author was a voluptuary"

There was a chorus of "Shame!" and then someone called out "Well, it's in a modern language anyway"

The speaker took no notice of the interruption. He was engaged in turning over the leaves and, after some moments during which the audience waited respectfully, he shut the book and said "I find that most of the stuff is about nightingales and things like that Are they much use to us? I think not I happened to notice also something about 'an unravished bride I call that rather dirty. What do you say then, boys? Shall we bung it in with the rest? Of course, I shall abide by your democratic decision."

"Bung it in, and damn democracy!" shouted the students, and they began now, without waiting for their spokesman's assent, to throw whole armloads of books on to the increasing fire. Although in the expression of some of the students the Professor seemed to detect some signs of shame or of reluctance, as a whole the flushed faces were strained and enthusiastic like the faces of those who are nearly drunk.

The Professor turned away He had been affected at first and immediately merely by the destruction of valuable objects Now he had a feeling of nausea in his stomach; for he was oppressed still more by the sight of the general degradation of spirit that made such destruction possible "I have inherited a civilization," he thought to himself, "but have failed to hand it on to posterity," and he wondered whether all the principles by which hitherto his life had been governed were to be proved false. Instantly he rejected the thought, but he was at a loss to know how such hatred could be inspired by works which to him embodied the soul of gentleness and sensitivity Of one thing, however he was now convinced. The civilization which, as Chancellor, he had endeavoured to maintain had been, at least in its upper strata and in its direction, generally corrupt Now he began to think of his son, of Jinkerman, and of their organization, of which he knew so little, as the only possible defenders not only of his own safety but of the idea of humanity and of the text of Homer. The terror which he had felt in the streets was being replaced by a more hostile determination which yet lacked an object With quick strides he walked up the hill past the University buildings Looking back he could see across the park and beyond the Chancellory the main thoroughfares of the city bright and, as it were, shrunken by the afternoon sun At this moment he heard the sound of guns firing a salute, and even at the distance at which he was from the streets, the noise of cheering and of bands

Straining his eyes he was able to make out near the triumphal arch from which the main avenue led into the centre of the city what was evidently the head of a procession So he stood and watched until he could distinguish clearly the bodies of cavalry, the beetle shapes of tanks, the gun-carnages and lorries proceeding at regular intervals, and behind them an indistinguishable grey mass of moving infantry These were the foreign troops who had been advertised as "deliverers" from his own tyranny, and now their presence in the streets seemed to him an even clearer mark of subjugation than had been the aeroplanes which in the morning had filled the sky He saw now unquestionably disappear his country's political independence and the liberties of his people ; for he knew that now nothing but revolution, a word which throughout his life he had regarded as most distasteful, could ever restore either the one or the other. He saw the long column of grey, boring, like a caterpillar or grub, into the entrails of the city, and though in reality everything had been determined since the morning he found a dreadful finality in the view

Nor was the reality of conquest diminished in his eyes by the fact that, from where he stood, the whole procession appeared tenuous, mechanical, and so small as to be almost ludicrous He was reminded of the sight of a toy railway which he had seen in the children's department at the Zoo, and the confused sound of voices which rose to him from the streets suggested the unreflecting and animal exclamations of young holiday-makers He thought of the passage in Lucretius in which the poet declares that from a view-point in the mountains the whole complication of an army's manœuvres in the plain will appear simply as a stationary shimmer of light The lines of poetry bore little reference to his actual situation He was not on a mountain but on the outskirts of his home: and below him was a grey army which, though its individual characters were blurred in the mass, had an order and a discipline and a purpose of which he was well aware Yet he was glad of his elevation, for it did at least detach him from the crowds of sympathizers below him and also from the other crowds who, he knew, in other quarters of the city were remaining in terror behind locked doors or even perhaps planning what could now be only a desperate and futile resistance The troops had now filled the main avenue, and smaller bodies were branching off the larger stream and parading up the other roads It was as though some fluid were being injected into the veins, altering totally the complexion of the city in which he had spent his life ; and as he watched the slowly spreading columns he felt indeed an exile, fancying that he had now been finally deprived of responsibility and that it only remained for him to escape, if he could, with Clara She, he reflected, was perhaps the only one among those whom he had known who, at this low ebb in his fortunes, would be glad to see him

He had been able as yet to make no plans for an escape, but now, as he hurried on towards the block of flats in which Clara's apartment was situated, he took from his pocket the piece of paper on which Jinkerman had written an address and was relieved to find that his next place of refuge was in the direction in which he was going, so that he would not have to retrace his steps through the more crowded part of the town. As for himself, he was satisfied with the security of his disguise, but he would find it difficult to escape notice if Clara were to accompany him. He began to consider what was the safest route between Clara's apartment and the house whose address had been given to him by Jinkerman, and he was still occupied with these reflections when he turned the corner into the shady square where Clara lived

Not wishing by his presence to incriminate her in any way, he had resolved to walk twice past the entrance of the block of flats before he would take the risk of going in. He followed out this plan and then, since the street and as much of the passage way as he could see was empty, he went in at the open door and began to climb the stairs Having reached the dooi of her apartment he paused for a moment with his ear against the wood, but could hear no sound from within. He turned the handle softly and by exerting pressure with his shoulder discovered that the door was not locked. He opened it and peered into the room

At first it seemed that the room was empty, but in a second theie was the sound of laughter and before the Professor had had time to withdraw his head two young men, dressed in the uniform of Legionaries and carrying wine glasses in their hands, came arm-arm out of Clara's bedroom, the door of which was immediately facing the door at which the Professor stood. The young men had seen him at once and the bigger of the two, still standing arm-arm with his colleague, shouted out "Hullo! You! What do you want?" The Professor smiled and prepared to withdraw, but the other officer had put down his glass on the table and now joined in "Stop a minute Just tell us what your business is here."

"I am a buyer," said the Professor instantly, "that is to say a seller of rags and bones" The next moment he wondered what on earth could have impelled him to make this selection out of a variety of possible occupations He added quickly, "And bottles," and the two Legionaries looked at him as though they were somewhat puzzled

At this moment Clara herself came from the bedroom She was dressed in a loose dressing-gown and carried in her hand a glass half filled with champagne "What's all the disturbance about?" she was asking in a voice that seemed somehow strange to him, The Professor took off his cap and, screening

with it his face from the others, winked at her in a conspiratorial manner But she seemed to have recognized him at once
She walked somewhat unsteadily to the table where she set
down her glass, then turned to the two Legionaries "Well,"
she said, "if it isn't my little Professor," and while the men
drew their revolvers from their sides she advanced to the door
and threw one arm round the Professor's neck. No action of
hers, not even if she had spat in his face or slapped it, could
have affected him more profoundly. He stood rigid, with his
eyes fixed on the flesh of her arm He did not hear the commands
of his captors to raise his hands After a short pause he began
absent-mindedly to pat her on the back

This gesture caused her to step away from him in surprise
She looked in his face and whatever she read there seemed to
arouse her hostility She stepped back unsteadily towards the
table and, supporting herself on it with one hand, looked at him
again with lowered head "Yes," she said, "it's true I don't
love you and I am a spy and I have betrayed you"

The Professor turned towards the two officers He had
nothing to say Clara leant farther towards him until he thought
that she was about to fall "Wait a minute," she said "I've
broken your heart, I suppose Well, what about mine?"

Again the Professor turned towards his captors, but one of
them jerked him back into the room "Go on," he said in a
low voice, "answer her"

It seemed to the Professor that he would not be able to move
his lips, but at length he pronounced the words "I do not fully
understand" He could see now that Clara was very drunk and
was not surprised when her voice rose to a pitch that was almost
hysterical

"What about my heart?" she was saying "What about my
man? Julius Vander, one of the best fellows that ever stepped,
killed by you and your police Do you think that because I
betrayed you I'd ever betray him? Oh no Do you think that
just because I'm a bit drunk now I didn't love him? Oh no!
He was a man He knew what he wanted He didn't talk
nonsense And he's dead, dead because of you, you blasted
thin-skinned ape, you silly dabbler, you old clergyman!"

She paused, and one of the two Legionaries nudged the
Professor in the ribs. "What have you got to say to that?" he
asked

"I have nothing to say," the Professor replied. Even behind

the vulgarity of her gesture and expression he still saw traces of the delicacy and sympathy that had made her congenial to him and successful, no doubt, in her work as a secret agent He found nothing strange in her preference for Vander over himself, but he could not see now where he would find another human soul to share his feelings.

Clara was looking at him intently "Oh God!" she said "Why must there be all this killing?" She turned abruptly away, entered her bedroom, and slammed the door. The two Legionaries took the Professor by his arms and conducted him down the stairs

CHAPTER XIII

ATTEMPTING TO ESCAPE

THE Professor's first thought when he entered the cell to which he was taken was, oddly enough, to see whether the narrow space contained a bookshelf and a writing desk. It contained neither of these articles

During the time in which he had been escorted through the streets he had been entirely unmindful of his surroundings and indeed would not have been able to say whether or not the officers who had arrested him had spoken to him on the way He did not even know in what quarter of the town his prison was situated, so deeply surprised and shocked had he been by the circumstances of his arrest. But now he began, as though for relief from speculations which oppressed him, to scrutinize closely the cell in which he was caught

The walls were whitewashed, but marked here and there with discoloured patches of dirt or scrawlmgs of pencil or chalk He examined these inscriptions and found them to be of an obscene character. The floor was of concrete and was damp as though it had been recently washed. A bucket in the corner of the room, and a bed, which consisted of a mattress laid on bars that projected from the wall, completed the furniture. The Professor passed his hand over the mattress and found that it also was damp He then turned towards the door and saw behind a grille, which was situated at about four feet from the floor level, a pair of eyes watching him

This sight so startled him that he relinquished his intention of climbing, with the support of the bucket, up to the small baried window that was set high up in the wall opposite the door Such an action, he felt, might be contrary to prison regulations; and so he sat down on the damp mattress and, taking out his pocket diary, began to write down the events of the long day that was now nearly over. He constrained himself not to raise his eyes to the door and not to think at all of his present situation, for he was dimly aware of the nervous condition in which he was and of the need which he might well have for all his fortitude and resolution

So for some time he wrote and was disturbed by no sound whatever from outside At the back of his mind, even while he was writing, he began to wonder whether he had been placed in an isolated wing of the prison or whether, what was most unlikely, only a few arrests had so far been made. Thus the sudden outbreak of noise, when it did come, was all the more startling He heard, as though it had arisen from nowhere, a clatter of feet in the corridor outside his cell and raised voices, but the sound had come so suddenly that he was unable to concentrate his attention quickly enough to hear the words that were being spoken The door of the cell next to his own was being opened, and after more noises of laughter, grunting, and scuffling, he seemed to hear something falling on the floor, quite close to the bed on which he was sitting, but separated from him by the wall, which, to have allowed the passage of the sound, must have been remarkably thin The cell door closed with a crash that shook the small electric light bulb that was fixed to the centre of his ceiling Then the clatter of footsteps died away as quickly as it had come The Professor looked down at the diary which was resting on his knee, but almost at once looked up again He could hear a low sound of moaning that seemed to come from close behind his back but which in reality must have proceeded from the next cell He listened intently, as though fascinated by the sound, and soon the moaning gave place to what might have been the noise of sobbing and tears, and what terrified the Professor most was the inhumanity of the sound Some man, he knew, an opponent of the regime, perhaps a Trade Unionist, perhaps a liberal, perhaps a scholar like himself, was suffering behind the wall, but from the noise he made it might have been a sick cow or horse

He rose quickly from the mattress and took two steps across the floor before he was arrested by the farther wall He turned to the door and saw through the grille the same two eyes watching him Now, regardless of what might or might not be the regulations of the prison, he fetched the bucket from the corner of the room, and placed, bottom upwards, below the window By climbing on to it he was able with outstretched hands to reach the bars that went across the small square of light, and with some difficulty he hauled himself up until his eyes were level with the aperture He could see nothing but the top of a wall from which projected an entanglement of barbed wire, and, on his right-hand side, the grey tiles of a portion of a steeply sloping roof His arms soon became tired and he lowered himself cautiously down to the bucket.

The sound from the next room continued to obtrude itself on his attention, and going over to the bed he listened to it intently for a few moments, then, turning round, began to rap on the wall, at first timidly, then with greater distinctness There was a pause in the curious and bestial moaning The Professor smiled and rapped again, for he fancied that the dull and indistinguishable noise which his knuckles made against the wall might convey some message of encouragement or of fellow-feeling And, indeed, though no reply was made to his signals, there seemed to him now to be something more restrained in the notes of the moaning and sobbing voice beyond the partition He sat now upright on his bed, having put away his diary in his pocket, staring in front of him, and from time to time turning to rap upon the wall

After some time he took out his watch and found that it was six o'clock in the evening While he was putting back the watch in his pocket, he heard once more the sound of footsteps in the corridor, and this time a sharp pang of fear seemed to pass through his whole frame. He listened as though his life depended on his catching up the minutest sound and it was with a sense almost of satisfaction that he heard what in reality he most feared, the footsteps stopping outside his door and the key turning in the lock He rose to his feet and his face assumed a grimmer expression as the door opened to admit four men, young and middle-aged, wearing the uniform of Legionaries

They closed the door behind them, and the Professor said almost before they had done so "I demand to know with what I am being charged, also that I be brought before a properly constituted judicial authority"

The men looked at him and one or two of them barely smiled

"Shut your mouth," said one who, from the stripes on the arm
of his uniform, seemed to be their leader. The four stood round
him and the Professor, looking into their eyes, saw nothing there;
but hostility, not even so much human feeling as might be
expressed by a show of triumph or a readiness to be amused

"Get down on your knees," said the leader of the Legionaries
The Professor hesitated, but could see no help for it but to
obey "Now get up again" The Professor rose to his feet.
"Now get down", and, staring grimly at him, the Professor
again obeyed As he looked at his persecutors he could see
that they were not even amused by the antics through which
they were compelling him to go. They seemed to be actuated
by a serious and efficient kind of savagery which to him was far
more dreadful than had been, for example, the behaviour of th
undergraduates who had burnt his books He began to fear
that they would soon attempt to make him deny his own friends
or applaud the change of government. This he was resolved
that he would not do, and he set his jaw, narrowing his eyes.

"Now stretch your arms out sideways," said the leader of
the Legionaries The Professor, kneeling on the floor, extended
his arms "Now take this," said the leader and with the words
he dashed his fist into the Professor's face This was a signal
to the others to fall upon him at once with boots, fists, and the
rubber truncheons which they wore at their belts It was not
long before the Professor collapsed beneath the hail of blows.
And if anyone who had known him previously had looked at
him after the four men had departed he would, apart entirely
from the change of costume, have found it hard to recognise
him For he was lying huddled in a corner of the room, his
spectacles broken and aslant his face, his lips curiously protruding, an effect which had been produced by the distortion of
the plate which held his false teeth, some of which indeed had
been knocked out and lay on the floor at his side. His forehead
was cut and bruised, blood also disfigured the lower part of
his face and his chest.

It was some time before he opened his eyes, and then for
some moments more he remained with his eyes just open, still
barely conscious. He felt the muscles of his flesh involuntarily
contract as though in resistance to some impending blow, and
he remembered where he was and what had happened to him.
When he attempted to sit upright the pain from his bruised sides
caused him to desist, and he contented himself at first by

gradually and painfully stretching out each limb to assure himself that no bones had been broken Then he succeeded in lifting himself up so that his back rested flat against the wall, and even began to search in his pockets for a handkerchief with which to wipe away some of the blood that he could feel round his lips and in his mouth He was now conscious of a dull pain that seemed to affect the whole surface of his body, and this continuous feeling served to, deaden both his intelligence and his pride. He was overwhelmed by an emotion of self-pity, and though the pain was not now unbearable he began to groan But no sooner had the sound escaped his lips than he remembered his fellow prisoner on the other side of the wall A thrill of pain shot up his neck as he turned his head towards the mattress on which he had been sitting He listened, half hoping that from beyond the wall he might hear some sound which would show that he was not alone in his suffering He heard nothing and reflected that perhaps his fellow prisoner had been removed to another cell. It then occurred to him that perhaps the man had died of the injuries which he had received, and he involuntarily moved his hand to his heart, causing a fresh spasm of pain to pass up his arm Very vividly to his imagination appeared the face of the dead Jinkerman, and he raised his eyes hurriedly to the door. Through the grille two other eyes were still watching him, but now this constant supervision caused him no embarrassment. He only dreaded to hear once more the sound of footsteps in the passage, for his whole body seemed to shrink from the proximity of human beings and from the very idea of pain

Indeed when, after some moments, he fancied that he had heard a sound in the distance he could not prevent himself from the beginnings of an involuntary effort to press himself, as though he could hide there, more closely against the wall The sound, if it had been a sound, ceased and he began to feel within himself the stirrings of animosity and of indignation Again a feeling of weakness overcame him and he closed his eyes Then, even in his extreme weakness, he reflected that what he had suffered so far was by no means all that he might expect to suffer. He had been brutally beaten but not made to feel the effects of any ingenuity of torture. Moreover, he could not possibly assess what would be the effect on him of prolonged confinement, of lack of contact with friends, of the coming and going in passages and in neighbouring cells, of the growing despair

which anyone in his situation was certain to feel Even now
he was straining his ears to catch the slightest sound, and he
knew that this constant attention to and preoccupation with his
fears could only end in madness

He began to search in his thoughts, as he had often done on
sleepless nights, for some familiar quotation or some passage of
literature which in the past he had regarded as both beautiful
and soothing In his memory the words of Alcman presented
themselves. "No longer, maidens with throats of honey, voices
of desire, are my limbs able to carry me," but to his astonishment
he could not recall the words in the original Greek He thought
of how he had last translated the passage in Clara's company
and was surprised to find that in his heart there was no bitterness
against the woman who, by her treachery, was responsible, at
least in part, for his present situation He picked up a piece of
broken glass from the floor and idly began to scratch the words
of Alcman upon the stone. He felt nothing but a dull pain,
extreme weariness, and some slight irritation at his inability to
remember the Greek words

Then his body stiffened again as he heard the sound of steps
marching in the corridor towards his cell He dropped the
piece of glass and directed his eyes to the door His face showed
both courage and determination, as though he had resolved not
to give in, but he could feel the tremor of his own body

The door opened and there entered the room not the four
men who had beaten him, but the two Legionary officers who
had arrested him at Clara's flat They stood for a moment at
the door surveying him with calm, but not altogether hostile
eyes Then the elder of the two went back into the passage and
whispered some order, the words of which the Professor could
not hear. The two men re-entered the cell and stood there
silent, looking about them as though the cell were empty.

Presently there was a knock at the door and there entered the
room an official whom the Professor took to be his gaoler and
perhaps the man whose eyes had so closely scrutinized him
during his hours of imprisonment He was a small man with an
indeterminate face, whose most pronounced feature was the blue
unshaven chin. He carried in one hand a bucket of water and a
sponge, and in the other a basket containing bottles, bandages
and lint As he advanced across the room it would have been
impossible to tell from his expression whether his feelings were
friendly or otherwise to his prisoner, but when, at his nearer

approach, the Professor had made a movement as though to withdraw himself the little man winked and smiled at him. This sight the Professor found inexpressibly delightful, and he remained quiet and at ease while his face was sponged and some of his wounds were dressed The gaoler then gave him a glass of brandy to drink and helped him to his feet, assisting him to take the first few steps which were painful enough to him Meanwhile the two officers had remained standing casually at ease, allowing their eyes to pass indifferently over the walls and furniture of the cell, as though they were gentlemanly tourists s uveying some antique monument

"Where are you taking me?" the Professor asked, and was surprised by the weakness of his own voice Neither of the two officers replied and, though from an abstract point of view their indifference to the plight of the prisoner might have appeared as disgusting as had been the conduct of the others who had physically maltreated him, the Professor at least was glad of their forbearance, and with no further questions followed one of them out of the cell while the other, holding a revolver, walked behind him

The Professor limped as he walked and at first found it necessary to steady himself by resting one hand against the wall of the corridor ; but, perhaps as a result of the brandy he had drunk, perhaps merely because his movement was no longer bounded by the walls of his cell, his mind was now clear, and for the first time he began to think of the injustice of his detention and of what steps he might properly take to ensure his release Justice, it was evident, was a matter of indifference to the new government, but he imagined that public opinion in foreign countries would be interested in his safety and thought already of the names of several distinguished figures who, in the Press of their own countries, would certainly demand for him a fair trial., Then he remembered that abject and broken moaning of the prisoner in the next cell, and he thought of the countless innocent and obscure men and women who at this moment were being tortured and lacked any means or hope of relief. His mind went out to Jinkerman and his son, and he wished them success, even in enterprises that would involve violence and civil war, so long as there was any hope of abolishing what to him seemed now the worst thing of all, a lawless and irrational oppression

The officer who preceded him had now reached the head of a

stairway. They descended the steps and halted in front of a large white door, at the two sides of which sentries were standing The officer knocked at the door, opened it, and motioned the Professor to go inside He entered, still limping, and found himself facing a large writing-desk at which was sitting, dressed neatly in Legionary uniform, the slender polite figure of Colonel Grimm

At the sight of the man the Professor's eyes hardened He thought of his Economic Plan, measures in defence of freedom which he had designed to be a model to the world, and he thought of his inability to assess either the cunning or the resolution of this policeman who had now sacrificed the independence of his country in preference to extending the possibility of a good life among his fellow citizens Since his spectacles had been broken he could not see the Colonel's face clearly, but he fancied that the man was smiling He stood still, waiting for the other to begin

"Please sit down, Professor," Colonel Grimm said, and when the Professor had done so he continued. "We meet under rather altered circumstances, and I can well imagine that your feelings toward me will not be exactly friendly May I beg you to give me credit for my own ideas of patriotism? All is fair in love and war, you know, and you will admit that I have as much right to my ideals as you have to yours"

The Professor, whose chair was quite close to the desk, observed the two quick smiles with which Colonel Grimm concluded his speech He made no reply, and after a pause the Colonel, with a trace of irritation in his voice, asked "I hope that you have no complaints to make of the way in which you have been treated?"

The Professor began to speak very slowly and in a voice which, because of its weakness, seemed most unlike his own "As you must know," he said, "I and no doubt many others have been treated abominably"

"I deeply regret it," said Colonel Grimm He waved his hand as though to dismiss a subject awkward, but of slight importance "These things," he said, "are unfortunately inevitable at these times But I need not go into that I can only hope that your experiences, regrettable as I find them, may induce you to listen more readily to the proposal which I have to make This, briefly, is what I am prepared to offer you We shall allow you leave this prison to-day and, after a short period of house arrest, to reinstate you in your position at the University In return for this we shall demand from you two written declarations first, that in the future you will refrain from any political activities, secondly, that you are on the whole convinced that in the present circumstances the policy of my government is the best one for the country The wording, of course, will have to be gone into We can phrase it as moderately as you like, so long as the general sense is clear" He paused and then, misinterpreting the Professor's silence, continued "I see that you are reluctant to trust our good faith Well, there is no reason why I should not tell you why we are making this offer In the first place we are encountering some unexpected opposition in some of the provincial towns This of course, can be dealt with, but a public declaration from you would strengthen our hand, and, incidentally, save some bloodshed Secondly, we anticipate a demand from abroad that you should be given a public trial That, as you can imagine, would be rather awkward for us. I hope I have now made the position clear I can assure you that you can rely on us"

"No," said the Professor slowly "I have seen too much already I could never do it." He let his head rest wearily against the back of his chair He was thinking of the alternatives to his acceptance of the proposal

Colonel Grimm looked him over coolly "Come, come," he said. "No doubt you are affected by some instances of apparent violence which have come to your attention You must be realist enough to know that this sort of thing is inevitable, though in point of fact our revolution has been accomplished almost without bloodshed Think of what would have happened if the revolution had come from the Left instead of from the Right Why, my dear fellow, it is too horrible to contemplate"

"No," said the Professor. "The violence then would have been rational, it would have been necessary, it would have had an aim But you are not aiming at more life You are killing the spirit" He stopped speaking, for he had no desire to argue, and in his own mind he felt a shock of surprise at finding himself, for the first time in his life, countenancing the possibility of a violent revolution.

"Let us keep to facts," Colonel Grimm was saying "The fact is that we are now in power and shall remain there. Further resistance will only lead to further bloodshed. Your support of our government would have undoubtedly a moderating influence, and would diminish that bloodshed I appeal, to you as a humanitarian"

The Professor looked at him gravely He reflected that this figure in front of him was also a man Careful investigation would no doubt reveal how and at what period he had first come to hate those ideals of human freedom, those principles of civilized conduct which, in the Professor's view, alone made life human and tolerable But at the moment he wished that the man could be wiped from the surface of the earth In horror he began to imagine the vision of Vander as a reality, a whole world governed in complete contravention of what to him had seemed the self-evident demands of reason, justice, kindliness, and fellow-feeling He saw himself as some pig-headed scholar clinging to the interpretation of a manuscript whose text has been proved corrupt, defective, or forged He thought again of his son's words "I hate because I love" and seemed to see in the words a dreadful necessity and truth Colonel Grimm was waiting for him to speak,' and when he opened his mouth he found it curiously dry "I must give you credit," he said slowly, "for some sincerity, but I can only hate everything for which you stand You cannot change my mind I reject your proposal"

A flash of anger appeared in Colonel Grimm's pale and discreet face "You realize the alternatives?" he said abruptly, and as he spoke again the Professor's flesh seemed to shrink as though it were some separate entity to which his mind was only loosely attached He nodded his head and Colonel Grimm pressed the button of an electric bell, summoning into the room the two officers who had escorted the prisoner to the interview. In the same order they went back to the Professor's cell where, without a word being spoken, the door was closed and the Professor left again alone

For some time he sat on the mattress, staring in front of him. His heart was beating rapidly, but not because of fear, rather because of a feeling of satisfaction, almost of relief, that now the die was cast Soon, however, he began to realize how little reason he had to feel satisfied either with his small and trifling protest to the authorities or with his own future He had imagined there to be something final in his rejection of Colonel Grimm's proposal, but now he saw that, should the government think it worth their while, all sorts of means might yet be employed to break down his resolution and to extort from him

the declarations which were desired. Or they might retain him
in prison without a trial, they might put an end to his life now,
in the next few minutes, or at some date in the future of which he
could never be sure Moreover, it was still possible that repre-
sentations from abroad might secure his release He had not
even the assurance of despair, could not even depend on the
certainty of either torture or death, but imagined extending
beyond the narrow walls of his cell a vast stretch of vagueness
and possibilities, a whole unexplored territory through which
he would have to go aimless and alone

Again he took out his diary and began to write slowly and
painstakingly, for he saw that his thoughts, liberated too far
from fact, could lead him only to terror and madness He
continued to write until it was too dark to see, and from time
to time looked up at the electric light bulb in his ceiling which
gave him no light. The bruises on his back and sides continued
to cause him pain, and finally he put his diary in his pocket and
lay down on his bed, without removing his boots, for the pain
which seemed now to increase rather than to dimmish made it
hard for him to believe that he would not again be soon molested,
and his feet were the only part of his body which so far had
escaped injury

He lay with his eyes closed and from time to time heard the
sounds of steps in the passage and the opening and shutting of
the doors of cells. These sounds were to him rather soothing
than otherwise, for what he most dreaded to hear was the sound
of blows or of voices crying out in pam. But he was still far
from sleep when suddenly the light in his room was switched on
and at the same moment he heard the heavy steps of several
men approaching his door He sat up quickly on his bed,
licking his lips and repressing the grimace of pain which the
sudden movement had caused him to make

The door opened and the four men who had previously
beaten him came into the cell The Professor sat without
moving, and the leader of the men said "Get up! You're
going out of here" With what dignity he could muster the
the Professor rose to his feet and accompanied the men out of
the room When he had heard the words spoken a sudden light
of hope for an instant irradiated his mind, but soon he began to
wonder whether these words might not be merely the prelude to
some new refinement of torture But as he went to the door he
could not have helped speculating as to whether, perhaps, the

efforts of his friends abroad might not have been successful, whether even it might not be possible that the government itself, convinced of his weakness as an opponent, had decided to connive at his escape. Outside the door was standing the little gaoler who had dressed his wounds and, as the Professor passed, the man smiled at him, but in such a way that it would have been impossible to tell whether the smile betokened commiseration or congratulation

They went down the stairs and past the door of the room in which the Professor had had his interview with Colonel Grimm Then, going through another door, they reached the open air, and crossing a space of ground came to the high wall, surmounted with barbed wire, which encircled the prison A gate in this wall was open, and through the gate the Professor could see the sky brilliantly lit with stars The four men stood at each side of the gate and invited him to pass between them "Where am I?" the Professor asked

The leader of the guard took a step outside the gate "You can see the University to your right," he said, and the Professor, following the direction of his arm, could distinguish rather below him (for the prison stood upon a hill) the lights of the big quadrangle which he knew He looked upwards and saw, far above his head, the constellation of the Great Bear His voice was curiously low as he asked "Am I free?" and he observed that the men were looking at him intently

The leader nodded his head and made room for him to pass, but the Professor did not move immediately His eyes remained fixed for a moment on the stars above the city, glittering with an unusual brightness through the cool night air. Then he stepped through the gate and looked at the lamps below him, to his right and left, uncertain which way to go He began to walk straight forward, slowly, and still limping, down the hill Perhaps his mind had already begun to turn with some hope to his son and to his few fnends, for he did not see that behind his back the guards had drawn their revolvers, nor had he proceeded for more than a few steps when he pitched forward on his face, the noise of a volley ringing in his ears, shot, as on the following day the newspaper reports declared, "while attempting to escape"

Printed in Great Britain
by Amazon.co.uk, Ltd.,
Marston Gate.